Mountain Base

BY MAX BROOKS

FOR YOUNG READERS

Minecraft: The Island

Minecraft: The Mountain

NOVELS

Devolution

The Zombie Survival Guide:
Complete Protection from the Living Dead

World War Z: An Oral History of the Zombie War

GRAPHIC NOVELS

The Zombie Survival Guide: Recorded Attacks

G.I. Joe: Hearts & Minds

The Extinction Parade

The Harlem Hellfighters

MOJANG
STUDIOS

MINECRAFT™

THE MOUNTAIN

MOJANG
STUDIOS

MINECRAFT™
THE MOUNTAIN

MAX BROOKS

DEL REY

NEW YORK

Copyright © 2021 by Mojang Synergies AB. MINECRAFT and the
Minecraft logo are trademarks of the Microsoft group of companies.
All rights reserved.

Published in the United States by Del Rey,
an imprint of Random House, a division of
Penguin Random House LLC, New York.

DEL REY is a registered trademark and the CIRCLE colophon
is a trademark of Penguin Random House LLC.

ISBN 978-0-593-15915-6
International edition ISBN 978-0-593-35528-2
Ebook ISBN 978-0-593-15916-3

Printed in the United States of America on acid-free paper

randomhousebooks.com

2 4 6 8 9 7 5 3 1

First Edition

Book design by Elizabeth A. D. Eno

To all the kids of Generation Lockdown.
May the rest of your lives be filled with great adventures.

THE FOLLOWING IS BASED ON TRUE EVENTS.

INTRODUCTION

If you've found this book, then you already know about the strange, block-built world around you. And if you've found my first book, you know about how I initially got to know it. You've already read about how I spawned in the ocean, all alone, near an island, and how learning to survive on that island taught me not only about this world, but about me as well.

And, if you didn't know that, now you do.

If this is the first book you've found, don't worry. I'll fill you in as we go along. All you need to know is that this story picks up where the other one left off, and while I thought I'd learned a lot already, I had no idea that my real education was just getting started.

MOJANG
STUDIOS

MINECRAFT™
THE MOUNTAIN

CHAPTER 1

Cold.

The feeling changed everything.

It'd been about a day and a half since I'd left my little block-shaped shore, and I don't mind admitting that I was barely seconds from going back.

It wasn't the first time I'd turned tail and run — well, paddled. A few days after landing on that strange, new land, I'd learned enough about crafting to accidentally produce a boat like the one I was riding in now. That time I'd been so inexperienced, so scared and frazzled and eager to escape, that I'd rushed right down to the beach and set off at full speed for the horizon.

And nearly gotten myself lost at sea.

This time, what felt like a lifetime later, I'd been determined not to repeat that same impulsive mistake. I'd spent a week provisioning myself for a long journey. I had plenty of food, tools, raw materials for crafting, and, most important, navigation aids like a compass and a nearly blank map. I say "nearly" because my little island appeared in the map's far east corner. And I mean "appeared." The moment I'd lifted it off the crafting table, the entire tan surface filled with a perfect, top-down re-creation of my island.

And me! I was on there, represented by a small white arrow that turned and moved along with me in real life. I remember thinking, *This is awesome, and with the compass, I'll never be lost!*

Following the manual I'd found in the mineshaft, I'd learned how to expand the map by surrounding the original copy with eight more pieces of sugarcane paper. I'd done it several times, until the island had shrunken to a little brown and green speck, surrounded by a thin blue ring and then a giant, blank space. So small in such a big, unexplored world. I still remember that mix of emotion, fear tinged with excitement. *What's out there?*

I'd have to wait another few weeks before finding out. That's how long it took me to write down my first book, leaving it to whomever might follow me. It was a record of all my adventures, and the lessons that came with them. And that last lesson was the one that drove me back to sea:

Growth doesn't come from a comfort zone, but from leaving it.

It sounded so cool at the time, so brave and true.

It rang in my head as I said goodbye to my animal friends, rowing west, turning occasionally to see everything I'd known fade slowly into the distance.

Smaller and smaller. Just like on the map. First went the low-lands, then the hill, then my house on top of the hill, and then, finally, the cobblestone observation tower that stretched far up into the clouds.

"Growth doesn't come from a comfort zone," I said, turning back to the now setting sun, "but from leaving it."

I don't know how many times I repeated that phrase, aloud and in my head, as the sun dipped, the sky darkened, and the pale crescent moon—*shaped like my island*, I thought with an odd pang of homesickness—rose behind me.

Hesitation.

There's gotta be land out there, I told myself. *Sooner or later, you'll spy something up ahead.* It wasn't fear that slowed me down. At least, that's what I told myself. *You don't want to miss something in the dark. Another island, low, and without a hill. It might be the start of a larger chain. Too fast and you'll pass right by.*

That's what I thought, scanning back and forth while being extra careful not to veer off course. The compass helped, its red-tipped needle pointing straight back to my original spawn point. The map helped too, filling in a straight, thick, unbroken blue line as I went, almost as if by magic. "No *land*," it silently told me, "*not yet.*" I thought about stopping altogether, taking a break, waiting for dawn. At least then I could be sure not to by-pass any land in the dark. I still wasn't one hundred percent sure that the map's vision was the same as mine. *If I can see even a little bit beyond what it marked . . .*

That's when I ran off the edge!

Of the map, I mean. Not the world.

The next time I checked, I saw that I'd paddled right off the western border of the paper. My interactive arrow was now a static circle. When had that happened? How long ago had I checked it? I should have been calculating distance and time, keeping track of the where and when.

And what if I DID run off the edge of the world? Didn't people used to think my world—my real, original spawn point—was flat? Didn't some dum-dums still insist that was true, even though a universe of evidence proved them wrong? But there was no evidence in this world, no proof that it was round. So much was different here: gravity, bodily functions, even time— each day's only twenty minutes! For all I knew, this ocean might just end at a giant waterfall, one that I couldn't see until I rowed right over the edge!

Don't freak out, I thought, *just make a new map . . .*

But of course, I couldn't. Maps needed a crafting table, which needed solid ground. *And it really wouldn't help*, I thought nervously. *The map only fills in where I've been. It can't tell me where I'm going. I have no idea where I'm going!*

Lost again!

No, I still had the compass. But that little metal disk nearly did more harm than good. The problem wasn't mechanical, but psychological, because, as I began to stare obsessively at the needle, I could almost hear it beckoning me home.

"C'mon," it seemed to say, "just follow me. No more unknown, no more worries about what might be out there."

I tried not to think of my island, my snug little cottage and soft comfy bed.

"Just follow me," said the compass, "and I'll take you right back to your safe space. It'll be so easy. C'mon!"

I knew the only way to keep those feelings away was to keep

them way behind me. I knew if I stopped, I'd turn back. And just like my last lesson had driven me to start this expedition, my very first one drove me forward.

Keep going. Don't give up.

And I didn't. I tried to keep focused on the here and now. Oars splashing, eyes scanning.

Something darted off to my right. A quick flash of black amidst white mini-cubed splashes. "Just a squid," I said, trying to comfort myself. "There are no sea monsters."

. . . at least none you've encountered yet.

Flat world.

Sea monsters.

"Just follow me home," taunted the compass.

As the moon set in front of me, and the first rays of the sun warmed my back, I couldn't believe I hadn't seen so much as a distant cube of land.

"Nothing?" I blurted to the empty expanse of blue. "Really? Nothing?"

There were no hints of salvation, like that first underwater mountain that had turned out to be my island. Nothing. The submerged hills below never came close to the surface. Not even a dry reef to stop and rest on.

"Keep going. Never give up," I chanted.

But for how long? How could I fight both my own doubts and the cop-out compass ganging up on me?

Maybe if I just turned back for a little bit. Not all the way home, just retracing my course, seeing if I missed some spot of land last night.

Keep going.

And what's wrong with heading back to the island? Take a few days to rest, start off in another direction.

Never give up.

There's three other directions, right? Three other chances to find something. That's not giving up. That's just restarting, rebooting, re—

Cold.

The feeling changed everything.

I'd still been moving forward. Slowly, but forward. And that bare minimum of motion had been enough to push me into a pocket of chilled air.

"Whoof," I breathed, feeling a slight chill run down my spine.

I slowed to a stop, letting every corner of my square brain switch on.

Was this a seasonal change? Do seasons change in this world? And if this was the first hint of autumn, wasn't it coming from the wrong direction?

My face was distinctly colder than the back of my neck. The two sides of my flat head were equally cool. So, this new rush of crisp air wasn't coming from north or south. Due west, directly in front of me. *How is that possible? Isn't climate supposed to get colder the farther north, and, I guess, farther south you go?*

Maybe in my world. But not here.

I thought back to another lesson from the island: Just because the rules don't make sense to you doesn't mean they don't make sense.

"Due west it is," I said, and started paddling slowly forward. I crept forward by inches . . . or, rather, by mini-cubes. I couldn't afford to miss anything now. I had to be sure that what I was feeling was real.

And it was.

The farther west I went, the cooler the air got. I did pause at one point, when, unexpectedly, I felt my face start to warm.

Did I pass through it? I wondered. *Was it some weird trick of the weather, a pocket of arctic air?* No. It was just the sun finally coming up to start shining directly in front of me. And as I started up again, I could feel those warm rays nullified by an overall plunge in temperature. I rowed all day, stopping only for a short lunch of baked potatoes. At least this world kept them eternally warm. I needed all the help I could get, because by the time the sun started setting, I was well and truly chilled.

My teeth chattered, and I wished this world would let me blow on my hands, or at least rub them together. It'd been a long time since I'd found any fault with the rules of my body or clothing. My crafted armor was great for protection against mobs, but in this cold I realized that the painted-on duds beneath them were no more than decoration.

If only I'd packed a sweater, I thought as the wind prickled my exposed skin. *If only I knew how to craft one.*

I might have had the materials to make warm clothes. I'd packed extra wool and some spider silk. *Maybe one of them, or both combined* . . . I stopped again, hoping that some mix of those items might come up with warmer clothing.

Big mistake. Not only could I not craft any winterwear, but stopping robbed me of any heat generated by movement. I also should have been more concerned with daylight, and not just for the warmth of the sun.

Darkness. Blindness. I had to slow, again, to make sure I didn't swish past the very thing I sought.

"Don't . . . think about the cold . . ." I shivered, as the night seemed to suck every last bit of heat from my body.

Fingers stinging, flat ears numb. Jaw aching from clenched, iron-tight muscles.

Don't think about the cold. Stay focused. Keep your eyes peeled for . . .

Land?

Something up ahead, a dark mass that hid the lowest stars.

"LAND!"

A hill, just like my island. No—more of them, spreading out the closer I got, and covered in white. Snow! It had to be!

"Aw yeah," I crowed, thrashing the oars about wildly. "Finally!"

Those were definitely hills, so many they stretched from one end of the horizon to the other. Not pure white, but mixed with lines of dark cubes.

Is that a tree?

I could see one, then several, sparsely scattered against a flat, pale beach.

"Yes," I hissed, "these ARE trees! This IS land! I've made it! I'm safe! I'm—"

I wasn't paying attention to what was right in front of me. My eyes were so focused on the hills and trees that I didn't quite notice the change in the color of the water. I didn't notice the thick, light blue crust that extended out from the shore.

CRASH!

I hit something hard enough to splinter my boat. I fell into the water, sank to the bottom.

Freezing!

You must know that feeling. That first millisecond when you plunge into the ocean, or a lake, or a swimming pool that you thought was heated and realize, too late, that it isn't? That was me, trapped in body-slamming shock.

I writhed for a second, let out a huge bubble of "Whhuuu . . ." as I shot quickly for the surface.

And hit my head!

The light blue water was hard.

Ice!

Panicked and punching! Mini-cubed cracks resealing with each blow.

Where was the edge?!

Looking around frantically in the dark. This way and that, swimming like a trapped fish. Lungs burning. Bubbles escaping from my mouth.

I couldn't believe it. Drowning, again. Clawing for the surface.

The stars above. My face pressed against the ice.

Air . . .

Can't reach!

CRACK! The first snap as the last of my lungs' breath vanished.

Pain, clear and cruel. And with it, clarity.

Panic drowns thought.

CRACK! Seconds left. But seconds used, not wasted.

The iron-tipped pickaxe on my belt. Now in my hands.

CRACK!

Bashing its tip against the ice. Giving way.

CRACK! SMASH!

Exploding up onto the hard, slick surface.

"Huuuuhhhhh." A deep animal breath.

For a second, I just stood there, because this world wouldn't let me lie down. Shaking in pain, too dazed to even see straight.

Hyper-healing. I'll never take it for granted. As my lungs recovered and my oxygen-starved brain cells restarted, I felt pain give way to hunger.

And thanks to this world, the food in my pack was, like me, insta-dry! Bread baked. Still warm, but not hot. Not enough to banish the chill.

What's that term when you get too cold and start getting sluggish — Hypertherm? Hypo . . . something?

Was it happening already? What did freezing to death feel like? I thought I remembered, vaguely, that it actually felt warm right before the end.

Which means I must still be all right, I thought, shaking violently between bites of bread. *If I am hypo-thermiating, I guess it's not in the final stages yet.*

But what about getting sick?!

You get cold, then you get a cold! Wasn't winter the time when everybody caught something? Didn't parents yell at their kids to dress warmly before going out to play in the snow? What could I catch? What diseases did this world have?

There was nothing on my island, but this was a whole new land! Hadn't that happened on my world? Hadn't explorers set off to discover new lands only to discover new illnesses? Hadn't some of those explorers wiped out whole civilizations because of the illnesses they brought with them? What did that mean for me? What if there were new sicknesses crawling around this new land, and my body was too cold and weak to fight them off? And if they were anything like being poisoned by a spider or a witch, or even that horrible gut storm I'd caught from eating the raw chicken that time—

"Stay focused," I said firmly to myself, gulping down the last of my hyper-healing fuel. "Stay calm."

I took a few breaths, forced myself to relax and to stop spiraling.

"Panic drowns t-t-thought," I chattered, moving my body to get the blood flowing. It worked, a little. I must have been generating just enough heat to feel my toes hurt. "That's it," I said between deep, calming breaths, "keep moving." A few more jumps, a quick run in a tight circle, and I could even feel the end of my nose.

"Calm down." I breathed slowly, feeling my body and mind release the tension I was building up with my panicked thoughts.

With calm came clarity, and with clarity came the method for calmly devising my next steps, which I called the Way of the Cube: Plan, prepare, prioritize, practice, patience, and persevere.

Prioritize. I need shelter! Both to get warm and, if nights here are anything like on my island, to get away from—

"Guuugh."

A familiar gurgling in the distance.

Oh no!

CHAPTER 2

I knew that sound, that burbling, gravelly growl. I spun to my left, looked down the beach. There it was, black against the snow, slouching slowly onto the ice.

"Guuugh!"

"Some welcoming committee," I sneered, reaching for my sword and shield.

"Guuugh." Arms raised, face lifeless.

Here's hoping these zombies aren't any tougher than the island type.

They're not. At least, this one wasn't. One sparkling swipe of my diamond blade sent it skidding across the frozen water.

"Here we go," I said, charging forward for a second blow.

I don't want to brag, but . . . well, okay, maybe I do just a little. But in case you didn't find my first book back on the island, you should know that I'd fought enough of these mindless meat bags to make sure Frosty the Deadman didn't lay one fetid finger on me. A few slashes, a final slice, then PUFF, I was standing over a rotting hunk of meat.

And to think, I thought, picking up the scrap of carrion, *that there was a time when I'd been so hungry that I'd actually lived on this stuff.*

"Is that it?" I shouted to the white hills. "Is that all you got?"

THUNK!

The arrow hit me square between the shoulder blades, knocking me forward onto the snowy beach.

CLICK.

CLICKETY-CLACK.

I turned just in time to take another arrow, right in the forehead of my diamond helmet. Its owner, a skeleton, was lining up his next shot when I raised my shield to block.

No problem, I thought, calculating how many shots I'd have to deflect before getting close enough to strike.

Then THOCK! Another arrow, this one into my right shoulder.

A second skeleton—no, two more—a little ways down the beach.

Then . . .

"Guuuggghhh . . ."

"Ssssp!"

CLICK, CLICK, CLICK.

My head swung in a quick circle, taking in the entire scene.

They were all around me. Zombies, skeletons, and those utterly terrifying spiders, their crimson eyes sparkling in the night.

How could I have been so careless, so arrogant! Mobs

spawned on darkened ground, and right now there was more ground than I'd ever seen!

How could I have forgotten it so quickly?!

Overconfidence can be as dangerous as having none at all.

CLICK.

"Ssssp."

"Guuugh."

RUN!

I headed for the only opening I could, a narrowing gap between two approaching zombies.

Inland, toward the hills.

WHOOSH! An arrow past my ear.

Zigzag! my mind screamed through the haze of fear.

Darting back and forth, practicing what had saved me so many times before.

"Guuugh!" A rotting hand reached out for me. *Dodge!* No time to hit back. *Go, go, go!*

I made for the shortest hill in front of me, with the easiest slope. Maybe I could find a cave, or even just a hole to block up behind me.

Up! Over dirt and rock.

THOCK! An arrow buried deep in the stone block next to my head.

Harder to dodge and climb.

A zombie hand reaching for my foot.

Higher! Almost there.

A spider's hiss, just behind me.

The summit!

I made it to the top, scanned the landscape before me . . .

. . . and discovered the true meaning of irony.

Way back, when I'd first climbed the stunted hill on that alien, angled island, all I'd wanted to see was more land. I'd hoped, prayed, that I'd reached the tip of a continent instead of a dust speck surrounded by sea. Now, here was my wish come true.

Frozen tundra stretched to the horizon. An endless white wasteland broken only by the occasional tree, or exposed rock, or roving, shifting shapes that couldn't be anything else but mobs!

Too much land. Too many threats.

What to do, where to go . . .

A light!

Far in the distance. Clear and bright. Not a star. It seemed reddish, orange. Maybe from a house?

Wait! There might be other people?!

"Guuugh!"

With no other option, I tore down the western slope, trying not to slip. I couldn't afford a twisted ankle now, even with my hyper-healing. No time to eat. I could see mobs converging on me from all sides. Fast spiders, steady zombies, the ever-clicking archers of bone.

And then . . .

I hadn't seen one until now, but there was no excuse not to have expected one.

Sssss . . .

A flashing out of the corner of my eye: a creeper just about to explode. I jumped, taking the blast in midair.

Shot away like a cannonball, I landed hard in a shallow ditch.

Ankles aching, ears ringing, the whole right side of my face feeling like it had kissed a furnace.

Keep going! Make for the light!

But where was it? Turned around by the explosion, and without the view from high ground, I'd lost track of it.

Use your head! I shouted in my head. *Don't panic.*

I rotated slowly, trying to find the hill. It was right behind me, which meant the light was directly up ahead.

I took off at a limp, which hyper-healed to a wobbly trot.

There it was again! Closer now! Growing with each forward step.

An arrow passed barely one mini-cube past my face. Another skeleton clacking from around a lone tree.

Keep going!

Dodging arrows, watching for creepers.

Enemies everywhere, even the ground! Yes, the ground. Up and down across unlevel terrain. Ditches and hummocks and now a river! Right in front of me, at the bottom of a gulley.

THOCK! Shot in the small of my back, tumbling down onto the ice below.

Pain, hunger. My hyper-healing spent. I got up, ready to keep running, then skidded to a halt as the snow before me moved.

The animal was large, white, and shuffling slowly on all fours. At first, I thought it might be . . . what . . . an arctic cow? No, too big, plus the small ears, black nose, and long, doglike snout . . .

A polar bear! It had to be. Had I read about them in that wildlife book I'd found? I couldn't remember. Probably not. I'd probably skipped that section on the assumption I'd never meet one.

Never assume anything!

And there wasn't any time to read the book even if I had it now instead of having left it back on the island for other potential castaways who might end up there! If this carnivore was as ferocious as the rounder versions in my world . . .

The bear swung its black-eyed face toward me. I switched from sword to bow.

Maybe a lucky shot, maybe two . . .

I drew back the arrow. Our eyes met.

Mammal eyes, like the animals who became my friends on the island. Cow and sheep. Warmth and feeling.

Just because someone doesn't look like you doesn't automatically make them an enemy.

The bear didn't move.

I strained at the bowstring.

"Okay," I breathed, "I don't want to kill you, and I really don't wanna be killed . . . but if you take the tiniest step closer . . ."

Whp!

An arrow streaked through the frigid night to bury itself in the bear's hulking mass.

Not my arrow! I'd already lowered my bow. The shot had come from behind me, from the skeleton on my tail.

"Frrmmf!" The snow-colored giant flashed red, turned toward me, and charged at a shocking speed.

"Whoa, whoa, whoa!" I yelped, dropping my bow in a sideways skitter. "That wasn't me! I didn't—"

But it was already past, taking another arrow as it raised up on hind legs to crash down on the doomed skeleton.

"Whoa," I whispered, watching in awe as the sheer brute force of this arctic predator utterly pulverized its tormentor.

That coulda been me . . .

As the skeleton poofed away, the bear swung back in my direction.

"Hey now," I said, picking up my bow. "We're good, right? You just fight to defend yourself? You seem pretty neutral, and since you obviously don't attack on eye contact like those creepy endermen, I bet we can get along just fine. In fact . . ." I started looking in my pack for food. *Do bears eat veggies and grains?*

"Are you hungry?" I asked. "Will food help you heal?" I swapped my bow for a carrot. "Sorry I don't have any meat or fish on me but . . ." I took a step forward, holding out my peace offering. "Would this work?"

Maybe we can be friends, I thought, just like Moo back on my island. *How cool would that be! With this bad boy as my traveling sidekick, we'd be a force to be reckoned w—*

Thk.

Thk.

Two arrows smacked into the ice between us.

"Maybe later," I shouted over my shoulder as I took off running. Two more skeletons came clacking over the lip of the gulley. Dashing back up the other side, I could see that a spider, three zombies, and a silent, gliding creeper were all in pursuit as well.

I couldn't depend on another bear-save. I guessed that arrow had been meant for me. No choice but to get away, make for the light, and hope against hope that it held my salvation.

Most mobs give up the chase after a while, and zombies couldn't catch up if I just kept running.

An arrow whooshed past my face, turning my head.

Another skeleton, off to my left.

But was it a skeleton?

Clothing. Or, rather, gray tatters hung over its bony form. Like the polar bear, this was new and unexpected.

As was the arrow that hit the heel of my left foot.

"Whhhhuuuut ttthhhhe . . ."

My speech slurred and my muscles locked up. Back on the island, a witch had splashed me with a potion of slowness. This arrow felt like it had done exactly the same thing.

"Oooohhhh c'moooon!" I verbally sloshed, trying to dodge as more arrows punctured my hip and arm.

Slogging, trudging.

I could hear the approaching zombies, closing the distance, helped by this new ragged skeleton. A team effort, or just some really bad luck?

Another slow arrow whizzing past me, buried in the snow, gray bubbles rising from its feathered shaft.

Keep dodging, keep going, keep your eyes on the growing light!

So close! Like a wall of orange, with the top much higher than any hill.

A collection of torches? I wondered. *A castle maybe?* In this world of armor and swords, why not! A castle with other people

like me! Armed and armored and ready to defend me from anything this cold dark continent can muster.

It has to be! I thought, feeling hope well up inside me. *Almost th—*

Lava.

I was close now. Close enough to make out that the bright
wall was just a river of molten rock.

I'd run all this way, been shot and socked, just to get within
sight of this world's version of a volcano.

I looked back at the approaching mobs.

"No, no, no," I sighed, "what else could go wro—"

I fell!

Right through the snow.

Right into a half-frozen pond at the bottom of a black, snow-
covered hole.

"Urgh!" I grunted, seeing that there was no way up. Too dark
to see. I groped in my belt for a torch, was about to stick it to the
wall, then heard the groans and hisses of the approaching mobs
above me.

DIG!

It wasn't a conscious thought, just pure instinct.

How many times in the past had burrowing saved my life?
That first battle with the first island zombie, and that last, final
time I'd been cornered and near death in the abandoned mine.

Dig, dig, dig!

Out with my shovel, into hard, cold dirt.

Down! Making steps, diagonally deeper.

Blocking them up behind me. Safe!

I placed a torch on the highest step, then turned back to the wall of soil.

"Not so bad," I said aloud, as my breathing slowed and my thinking sped. "This is what I was going to do originally, right? Back there on the beach. Dig a shelter, sleep till dawn. No problem."

After a rejuvenating snack of carrots and bread, I began to hollow out a small three-by-three chamber with just enough headspace to stand.

"Okay," I said, setting down the premade bed. "By morning the mobs'll burn away and I can get a better look at where I am."

Slipping under the thin red sheet, I yawned. "And sleep is just what I need right now. Rest my body, rest my brain." I felt my eyes drift closed. "Be nice to finally get some sleep."

But I didn't.

"Guuugh." The zombie moaned through the dirt. It was right overhead, barely a few blocks above me, and there were more mobs showing up. I didn't know if they were the ones that'd followed me or if they'd newly spawned. But it sounded like a heck of a party up there. Clacking and hissing, and, I'm sure, silently gliding like those creeper bombs do.

Can they blow up without seeing you? I wondered. *If they've got different types of skeletons here, then maybe there's a different kind of creeper, too.*

"Sssp." I jumped at the spider's hiss, picturing those red target sensors staring right through the earth toward me.

Calm down. Think!

If they wanted to get me, they would have done it by now.

More moans, more hisses.

I knew they couldn't get me, but I repeated "You can't get me!" out loud to the earthen ceiling.

"Guuugh," moaned a zombie, as if to say, "Maybe not, but we can sure keep you up all night."

"That's what YOU think!" I barked at them. Jumping out of bed, I punched it back up into my pack, then started shoveling away at the dirt floor.

"Deeper!" I called to the monsters above. "Just a little deeper and safer so you can't mess with my head!"

And I knew it was all in my head. I knew I was making myself crazy with nerves. But if the solution was as simple as a deeper hole, why not go that way instead of trying to calm myself down all night?

As dirt gave way to stone, I chirped, "Perfect," and exchanged my shovel for the pickaxe. "Even creepers can't blast through a couple layers of solid rock."

A short time later, I had a hollowed-out bunker. With cobblestone sealed up behind me, I set my torches on the wall, my bed back on the smooth, hard floor, and jumped right in for a good night's rest. Safer, and even warmer from all the built-up body heat. A final baked potato to make up for those calories lost, and now, mentally and physically, I couldn't have been more satisfied.

Made it, I thought, snuggling under my blanket. *Made it to a new land, made it past an army of monsters, and now I'm finally ready to continue my quest.*

Another yawn, eyes closing.

Tomorrow's gonna be a good day. I might even find my way home . . .

CHAPTER 3

Cold!

Again!

And this time it was worse than when I first rowed into it.

This time, I woke up shaking, chilled right down to my bones.

"Whoof," I gasped, jumping onto the icy floor. Tight muscles, spasming limbs. "Whubu-huh-hasubusah," was all my chattering teeth could say.

Of course—I should have planned for this! All that built-up body heat couldn't last! Lying still all night, surrounded by warmth-sucking stone. I could have at least laid down a furnace, thrown in coal and all the extra cobblestone I'd gotten from building this underground refrigerator.

Maybe, I thought, punching up my bed and heatless torches, *I'll just lay down a plank of wood and set it on fire with a flint and steel. Just enough flames to warm my face and hands.*

But I realized I couldn't stay hidden underground burning my supplies—and burning daylight! Given how short the days were in this world, I couldn't waste one more minute in this hole.

"T-t-time t-t-to g-go," I stuttered like an old-timey cartoon character. "At least-t-t the sun'll k-keep me w-warm . . ."

I broke down my cobblestone "door," marched up and into my earthen room, collected the torches I'd left to keep the mobs at bay, and prepared to break down the dirt wall.

Click, click, click. I stopped, hearing the skeleton on the other side.

"Aw no," I said through frozen earth. "Not this time. You think I don't know what you're up to? Waiting there in that shaded little pond hole, safe from the sunlight, hoping I'll be dumb enough to just come blundering into your arrows."

"Click, click, click," came the response, which had to be, "Uh, yeah?"

"Well, it ain't gonna happen," I answered, and turned my shovel on the opposite wall. "I'll just tunnel the other way, up into the bright, safe sun."

I dug out a stairway to daylight. I could almost taste the rays on my face, banishing the cold, bathing me in hot, welcome . . .

"Oh c'mon!" Breaking through the earthen roof, a small, diamond-shaped flake of four mini-cubes came fluttering slowly onto my face. A snowflake. It was snowing up there.

"Come on!" I whined, climbing up into this world's version of a blizzard.

So much for being warmed by the sun. Each flake felt like a stinging, icy needle on my skin. An assault by nature itself! "What did I ever do to you?"

Click, click, click.

The skeleton. Laughing at me from . . . Where was the hole?

Turning in its direction, all I saw was unbroken ground. There had to have been an entrance last night. How else could I have fallen through it?

The snow didn't help, obscuring my vision with its curtain of infinite sting-flakes. I should have just backed up, left it alone, gone on with my journey and remembered my rule about *careful curiosity*

I actually thought I was being careful as I stepped gingerly forward, eyes on the ground, ears guided by the invisible, incessant clacking. I was sure I'd see the hole in front of me any second.

Whoosh!

Right through the snow!

I fell back down into the cave and into the freezing pond.

Thock! An arrow in my chest, and the gray, lipless smile of an approaching skull.

I raised my shield, deflected the second shot, then swung my sword and felt dry bones crack against the edge of my diamond blade. The skeleton must have already been weakened by the morning light. It turned to smoke before I could swing again.

"What the . . ." I started to say, looking up at what appeared to be a solid white ceiling. It was thin, no more than a mini-cube at most. What was this, quicksand . . . or quicksnow? How could I fall through something without even leaving a mark? And when I tried to touch that ceiling—just one punch, mind you— the whole roof spontaneously shattered.

"New land, new r-r-rules," I said as a chilled bolt shot up my spine. In the "heat" of battle, I'd forgotten that I was standing in waist-deep, ice-cold water.

Get moving, get warm.

Digging out a staircase to the surface, I poked my head out with renewed caution. There might be other mobs waiting for me there, protected from the morning sun by the heavy gray sky overhead.

I made sure to scan the horizon, looking for anything moving on its own. There was that polar bear from last night, shuffling around as if its recent battle had never happened. There was what looked like a creeper, but so far away I couldn't be certain. And there were a few of those little, hopping dots, barely visible between the falling flakes.

I can't tell you how disconcerting that moment was, trying to make out shapes from far away. Back on my island, everything had been so close. Even down below in the lava canyon, and below it in the abandoned mineshaft. Nothing had ever been farther away than a couple dozen blocks.

Now, in this vast expanse, I almost felt lost at sea again, but with a whole new assortment of shapes and threats to identify. And now my only ally, the sun, had taken a holiday at the worst possible moment.

Back down to the bunker? I wondered. *Light a fire, have breakfast, and wait for the snow to stop, even if that means holing up for another day?*

As I weighed that increasingly attractive option, my tortured eyes swung into view of the volcano. Red, glowing. Close enough to reach in a few minutes.

If I'm looking to warm up, I reasoned, *that's a whole lot hotter than a furnace. And once the snow stops, climbing to the top will give me a better view.*

It wasn't exactly the rousing start to my day that I'd hoped for. My nose burned from the cold, along with my ears and fingertips. And my teeth chattered so hard, I thought they might actually crack. I couldn't feel my cheeks, or rather, I felt like there were thick, heavy pads glued to my face. That's what happens when you lose all feeling in them. That's how my toes felt as well, no matter how hard I tried to wriggle them.

Will I lose them? I wondered nervously. *Isn't that what happens to people who're out in the cold too long? What's the term for that?*

Frostbite. The metaphor for being attacked by the cold. *Will hyper-healing fix frostbite?* I wondered, blinking red, raw eyes.

Something darted off to the side. Something small, fast. A silverfish? A surface-dwelling version of those tiny foot nibblers? Another one, in front of me this time, just beyond a small hummock. Sword ready, I charged!

And came face-to-face with nothing more than a black and white bunny rabbit.

"Whew!" I breathed, and then, with a twinge of embarrassment, said, "Sorry if I scared you. I guess I'm a little jumpy."

The rabbit wasn't listening, too busy bouncing back and forth through the snow.

"Hey," I said, reaching into my belt for a carrot. "You hungry?"

But it was too far away to notice, as it hopped away over the pale expanse.

"Hey, look," I called, trying to catch up.

Quicksnow!

The thought of falling through one of those invisible traps slowed my steps. "Hey, hopper," I hollered again, waving the orange root. "Look what I got for you!"

The rodent ignored me, vanishing through the falling snow.

Two for two, I thought morosely. *First the bear, now the bunny. No luck yet with making any new animal friends.*

At least I was closer to the volcano, and with each approaching step, I could feel the increasing, welcome heat.

I sighed at the prickling sensation of what had to be blood returning to my frostbitten skin. At about ten blocks I stopped and just absorbed the heat. I could feel it on my face and arms, and, after a few thawing moments, there was even a tingling in the ten little icicles that used to be my toes.

"Mmm . . ." I sighed again, and turned around to give my back its turn. That acted like a heated highway for my whole body. In a few minutes I nearly felt human again, and raising my temperature was almost enough to raise my spirits.

I say "almost" because turning back around to face the lava brought a lot of chilling memories. The most immediate one had to do with what happened to my first house. How I woke up to find the creeper in my living room, to hear the explosion, to see the lava cubes from the hot tub I'd built upstairs spilling out and down my little hill.

"Enough," I said aloud, trying to shake off the memory as I stepped gingerly around the bubbling red pond. "Keep focused."

And I did, looking for the safest, easiest slope to climb. I walked around the lava's perimeter, looking for caves as well as a way up. I worried that any shady shelter might conceal another waiting mob. After falling through the snow, I couldn't afford to relax. But I didn't see anyplace where a monster could hide. And, ironically, the only way up I could find was right back where I started. Right next to that lethal stream, the slope seemed to rise in a naturally occurring staircase.

"Careful," I told myself, "careful . . ."

I kept my eyes, and mind, fixed on every step ahead. The slope was nearly barren, not a tree or clump of grass in sight. The only thing growing was a single red flower barely two blocks away from the lava stream. "You're braver than I am," I told the little poppy, and then noticed something unusual about it. I thought I remembered, but I couldn't be sure, that I'd passed other flowers that only grew in groups. I tried looking behind me, but through the snow, it was hard to spot any more plant life.

I also noticed a weird little quirk of this volcano—the lava poured out from the side. About a third of the way up, right next to the lone poppy, I saw that the source of the stream was a single cube space in the rocks. Weren't they supposed to come from the top? I didn't know. After all, I don't think I was a geologist, or volcano-ologist, or whatever you call those folks back in my world. For all I knew this side-flow was perfectly normal in both worlds, and the only reason I've taken an entire paragraph to bore you with this question is because it's gonna come into play later.

Just like the smell.

I barely noticed it at first, just the faintest whiff, but as I climbed farther up, I could swear my nose detected something . . . unusual? I tried a couple deep inhales, but the cold, dry air only made my nostrils hurt. It wasn't the lava; I was sure of that. It was coming from someplace farther up. It smelled like . . .

Okay, now, fair warning: If you're super-sensitive to words, skip this paragraph. But I'm telling you, this smell, this growing stink drifting down toward me, could only be described as that word that's created when F meets Art.

Yep, I said it. Okay? Sometimes truth is rude, but that's the plain truth of what I was smelling. "Do volcanoes toot?" I asked myself aloud, and nearly fell backward at the audible CLICK that answered.

CLICK.

What was that?

I paused, spun, reached for my sword, and, again, almost fell right back down the slope. I thought it might have been a skeleton, although experience had taught me that the sound couldn't have been any more different. This wasn't the rapid CLICKETY-CLACK of bones. This was just one quick, high-pitched CLICK.

And then it was gone. And so was the unpleasant smell. Had the wind shifted? No, that doesn't happen in this world. Had I moved up past it? Probably, I reasoned. But what had been the original source?

A crack between the stones? I'd learned that sometimes diagonal blocks have just the tiniest space between their edges. Raindrops through my island house's slanted roof taught me that. Maybe that was the case here, an imperceptible slit between two stone blocks that was giving off that impolite odor.

It was a mystery to be sure, as was the hole I discovered a few blocks up.

Just one block in size, pointing out sideways like the lava opening. I peered inside, and saw that it went far back into darkness. I thought about maybe planting a torch inside for a better look, or even going to work with my pickaxe to see if it led to a larger cave.

Don't get distracted, I reminded myself. *For all you know, that's just another lava hole ready to erupt, and besides . . .*

I looked up at the inviting summit.

You're almost there!

A few slow, nervous minutes later, I was standing at the top, and for once, luck was with me. The snow stopped falling, the sun came out, and I got my first clear look at the world around me.

"Thank you," I said to the sun, closing my eyes and letting my face warm for a second. "Good-luck mountain," I breathed, then opened my eyes to take in the view. I was facing east, toward the rising sun, and from this height, I could see all the way to the coast. There was the ocean, barely visible past the chain of low hills, and that thick, pale ice crust that had wrecked my boat. There was the "quicksnow" hole I'd fallen into. And there was the frozen, purplish river I'd crossed, with, yes, my polar bear ally still muddling about at the bank.

Turning in a slow, three-sixty arc, I realized that this barren wasteland had a kind of beauty to it. The hills and valleys, the frozen ponds and occasional trees with their pointed, dark green leaves. And there were more red flowers, and even a few yellow ones, and yes, they were all in clusters that broke up the snow.

"Not bad," I said, "not that I'd want to live he—" Just as I finished my full rotating view, I noticed a total, dark break in the western horizon. It was so far away, I might have missed it if the snow had been falling. Another snaking, iced-over river, and beyond that . . .

A forest! Yes, a real, honest-to-goodness forest, so vast it stretched from one end of my vision to the other.

"Here we go," I sighed, then repeated with more excitement, "Here we go!"

Picking my way down, I had to force myself to go more slowly. "Careful!" I repeated, resisting the urge to jump. "Care—"

Click!

There was the sound again!

Click!

And again. Behind me!

I turned but couldn't see anything. I scanned the slope I'd just come down. Nothing. I looked left, then right. Everything was quiet, still. Nothing but stone, dirt, and occasional lines of gravel.

Sword up, I twisted, ready.

Crunch.

Another rabbit, with pink eyes and fur as white as snow. "Oh, that was you," I said. "*You've* been making those clicking sounds. And"—smiling at my own cleverness—"I bet that little hole I discovered was your burrow." It felt good to finally be getting a handle on everything, to understand the rules of this new land.

At least that's what I thought.

"And, hey," I said as I reached again for a tempting carrot, "you know you want this, right?"

I couldn't mess this one up, not with the animal right above me. "Mmm, nice." I waved the morsel before its small, attentive face. "Let's be pals, okay?" It looked at me as I stepped closer.

"That's right, c'mon," I said, already envisioning our new, lasting friendship. "I think I'll name you NO!"

That last word came as the bouncing squeaker jumped right off the cliff past me and crash-landed into life-ending smoke.

"Ohmywhat?" I gasped, running to a patch of hovering fur and meat. "What were you thinking, you dumb bunny?" I asked the remains hopping into my pack. "What kind of world lets that happen?!" I remembered when my animal friends back on the island blindly loped toward the lava from my house, the chicken roasting itself alive.

The memory didn't console me; it only reminded me that this was the rule of life in this world. It didn't help that this was an accident. It just hurt to watch something, anything, innocent die.

I had no idea that this small death was nothing compared to the savagery that was waiting for me in the forest.

CHAPTER 4

The closer I got to it, the more I could smell the forest, which was a nice change from the sterile, stinging air of open tundra. Even with the wind at my back, I got pleasant whiffs of bark and . . . pines? The hint of sap, the faint reminder of cleaning products from that other world. And . . . a holiday as well. A big one. I'm not sure if I celebrated it back home, but a whole lot of other people did. And those memories drifted just out of reach with the smell of the trees up ahead.

The forest was vast, mysterious, and inviting. I quickened my pace, practically skipping past what I thought at the time was a huge drift of snow blocks, and crossed the second frozen river into the woods.

Getting closer, I could see that they were, in fact, a version of pine trees. Spruce, specifically, which I'd previously read about in one of the manuals. Some were short, stubby little dwarfs, others rose high above my head. Brown trunks and green, square pine needles. Dark colors, concentrated. Like they were trying to hold in their color the same way I was trying to hold in my body heat.

And so many! I'd chopped down every last birch tree on my island, then replanted them, then chopped down and replanted them again just to build my first mansion. Now, I could build ten — a hundred — homes without making a dent in this forest! And they weren't alone.

I noticed what at first looked like saplings growing here and there, but when I reached down to pick one up, I saw they were this environment's version of grass. Squat and triangular, some crunched into nothingness while a few yielded very familiar seeds. *Will this grow into wheat,* I wondered, *or some new kind of plant?* I pocketed the seeds, then tried harvesting something from a taller, fernlike bush. I didn't get anything, but I didn't need to. I was looking for answers, not food.

And one question I needed answered was whether creepers could lurk in the shade of these trees. If the little birch grove on my island could have hidden living bombs — which had almost killed me then — how many legions could be lurking under this expansive canopy? And it didn't help my nerves that my visibility extended barely a few blocks in front of my face. Between the dense trees, the grass, ferns, and rolling terrain, I had to be on my guard.

Always be aware of your surroundings.

Senses heightened, shield ready, I crept slowly through the right-angled underbrush. *Even if I don't run into a creeper,* I reasoned, *there might be an easily startled polar bear over the next ridge, or maybe a brown version that's not as friendly, or some other animal I can't even imagine just waiting among the bushes.*

How right I was.

"Woof!"

I jumped, not believing my ears.

"Woof!" Again, right over the next rise. A dog?!

"No way," I said, and rushed forward with a beating heart.

A dog!

It had to be! A new friend! Brave, trusting, and loyal to the end! I mean, c'mon, what better pal is there in this or any other universe . . . unless you're a cat person, I guess. Sorry. But I'm a dog person . . . At least, I think I was, back in my old life. Why else would I have been so excited, and why else would I have been just the slightest bit disappointed to crest the hill to find an animal that could technically be called a dog, but not the kind you'd want to snuggle on the couch with.

This animal was speckled gray, with a narrow tan snout, upright, black-lined ears, and a tail that was definitely not wagging.

A wolf. Of course. I'd read about them in the wildlife book. But, as with the bear, I hadn't bothered to study any passage about anything that wasn't right in front of my face.

"Um, hi, boy," I said, taking a cautious step forward. "Hi . . ."

It darted forward. I instinctively retreated. But instead of attacking, it simply looked up at me, barked again, then turned and trotted away. "Hey, wait up!" I called, hopping after it, "Uh . . . sit! Stay!" For the third time in this cold, crazy land, I reached into my pack for some food.

"You hungry, buddy?" I asked, dangling the rabbit carcass in front of its nose. "You know you'll like this."

I might as well have been holding up a rock.

Gotta be something else, I thought, *another kind of food or . . .*

"Stick!"

A log block from my pack gave me four planks, which in turn gave me eight sticks. I held one up, ready to throw.

"Go get it, boy!" I shouted. "Go on!"

Chucking one of the thin batons far over its head, I cheered, "Go for it! Look! C'mon! Go!"

No.

The wolf just stood there, staring at me with a quizzical expression that had to mean "You gotta be kidding." Then it turned and walked away, leaving me alone once again.

"What's it gonna take?" I huffed, stomping over to retrieve my stick. "What's it gonna take to make a friend around here?!"

"Bah."

I knew that sound; no way could it disappoint.

"Baaah."

"A sheep!" Just over the next hummock. And sure enough, not only one, but a whole herd . . . or flock . . . or whatever you call them. Half a dozen! Grazing peacefully in an open patch of snow.

"About time." I sighed, feeling like I'd just found an old friend on the first day of a new school.

"Bah!"

"Wow, am I happy to see you guys!" I breathed, but then added softly, "I'm a friend; I mean you no harm."

They might have been sheep, but they were still strangers. I climbed slowly down the rise toward them, not sure if this forest variety was more skittish than my island pals. They didn't seem to be afraid of me, or notice me for that matter. Just like the island type, they were content to randomly munch the ground at their feet.

There were a couple black ones like Coal and white ones like Cloud, so bright I almost missed a few against the snow, and gray ones . . . so many different shades of gray! From the barest off-white to dark, nearly charcoal to the middle hue that made them perfect ringers for little Rainy, the lamb I'd helped bring into the world by feeding her parents wheat.

And there was a brown one! Mixed in among all the others, with a unique rich coat that reminded me of a milk chocolate bar.

Chocolate.

The thought of my old world's luxury made my mouth water, and as I reached into my pack for some bread, I remembered that I'd packed the raw ingredients for bread that, I was sure, would make me the star of a whole new woolly fan club.

"Hey." I stepped up to the brown sheep, holding out a handful of blond, ever-ripe wheat. "This look better than frozen grass?"

"Bah!" Heads went up. All of them! And before I knew it, I had a multicolored stampede on my hands.

"Whoa, whoa"—I gulped as woolly faces nuzzled me from all sides—"don't crowd!"

I should have put this new rule in the old book: Don't offer what you got unless you're ready to share with everybody!

"One at a time," I demanded, trying to think about how I was going to feed them. In addition to sheer numbers, there was now the issue of who goes first. As I knew from my time on the island, giving the sheep some wheat would quickly create new lambs with a bunch of different color combinations. And who was I to choose the look of this flock's next generation?

"A lot of power," I breathed as they continued to nudge me back, "a lot of responsibility."

"Baaaah," they bleated impatiently, as if yelling, "Can ya just get over yourself and feed us already!"

"All right, fine!" I groused, deciding on the most basic method. First come, first served.

I started feeding whoever was in my face, and wondered if this world could let that face redden. With hearts flying and lambs popping, it was all I could do not to close my eyes.

"Bah! Bah!" Little, high-pitched calls mixed with deeper, parental bleats. Five little lambs in all: two white, two gray, and a cute brown one that reminded me of a little chocolate chip. "Happy Birthday, Chippie," I said, and offered the baby and its siblings their own helping of wheat. "I know you're just an animal and I know you can't really understand what I'm saying, but, on my side, this meeting is the best thing that's happened to me since landing here."

Little Chip just looked up at me, its small black eyes filled with wonder. "'Cause," I continued, "if I found you, maybe I can find other animals to bond with as well. Maybe . . ." I hesitated at saying "chickens," experiencing a twinge of guilt at the memory of losing my last chicken friend. "Maybe a cow. Like my friend Moo, back on my island. You'd love her. She was . . . is . . . the best."

"Bah!" Chip answered, and bowed its head for a helping of snowy grass.

"Yeah, I get it. You've been patient with me long enough." I noticed that now that the wheat was gone, the gathering was breaking up, spreading out among the trees.

"You got places to go, and I got a continent to explore."

"Bah!" replied Chip before ambling away.

"See ya around, kid," I said, turning back for the west.

With a renewed sense of confidence, I strode happily over the next ridge. Meeting the sheep had calmed me enough to get the old brain thinking rationally again.

I should probably make a new map. No sense in all this exploring if I don't make a record of what I find.

I was just going over my stock of iron, redstone, and sugarcane paper when I heard a lone "Bah" back over the last rise. I wouldn't have thought much about it, but that bleat was followed by a quick, familiar bark.

"No," I whispered, feeling my blood grow colder than the air. "No, that can't be happening. You're just making assumptions from your own world."

And yet, there I was, walking, then running, back the way I came, back over the blocky ridge and looking down at the empty grazing patch.

Almost empty.

Two objects were hovering over the bare snowy turf: a block of white wool and a leg of reddish pink meat.

"No, no, no," I cried, rushing over to pick them up. It had to be an accident. The sheep must have fallen off the ridge, like the dumb bunny earlier. It couldn't be . . .

"Bahh . . . Ruff, ruff . . . Baaahhhh!"

Beyond the nearby trees. Sounds. Movement.

I raced over just in time to see the wolf pounce on a gray-colored sheep. A flash of red, a loud, pained "Bah," and Rainy's double was poofed into meat and wool.

"No!" I yelled, watching in terror as the carnivorous canine moved on to the little brown lamb. "Chippie!"

Running, sword drawn.

"Bah!"

A flash of diamond blade.

The wolf flew back with a startled yelp.

"Get out of here!" I shouted to Chip. "Go on! Run!"

SNAP! Pain on my armored leg. Turning to see wolf eyes now glowing red.

"Grrrr."

Another snap, blocked by my shield.

"Get away from them!" I yelled, raising my sword.

Another growl and another blocked snarling bite.

"Get away!" I swung, knocking the animal against a tree.

It yelped, then smoked into a silent puff.

"I'm sorry," I breathed, adrenaline ebbing into sadness. "I didn't want to kill you. I know you were only following your nature, but I couldn't let you . . ."

"Grrrrr."

Something struck me from behind, smashing my face into a tree.

"Wha . . ." I turned to see three more wolves, their eyes seething red like giant spiders.

Of course, I thought, cursing myself, again, for not having studied the manual. *Wolves run in packs!*

The first one jumped, so I sliced. Its yelp was drowned out by the growls of the other two as they lunged. I grunted as teeth sank into my left leg and right arm.

"Back," I yelled. Blade swishing, chopping sideways. "Back!"

My cries were cut off as the first wolf leapt at my back. I turned to face it as the other two jumped at me again.

Slash, block, bite.

Outnumbered!

I could feel the rending teeth, jaw-power capable of breaking bones. I retreated, swinging wildly. The pack closed. I ran.

Lead them away, I thought, dodging trees and hopping rises. *Lead them away from the sheep, get them far enough away before turning to fight.*

My hyper-healing kicked in, replacing pain with hunger. It wasn't enough. I'd need to rest, to eat.

Their snarls were behind me, closing in fast. Locked like guided gray missiles. I could see the end of the tree line up ahead. Maybe they'd stop at the wood's edge.

"Grrrr!"

Maybe not.

Barely steps ahead of snapping jaws, I burst through the trees and tumbled down onto the frozen river.

"Grrrr!" A bite on my hip, sending me skidding across the ice.

Get up! Get across! Get to . . . to where?

That big clump of snow I passed earlier. Only it wasn't a clump! From this angle, I could see. . . . a *door*? Yes! There was a door right in the middle of those white blocks! What did they call those huts in the far north of my world? Igloos? Whatever! It was my only refuge!

Running with all my might, leaping in, slamming the door behind me, and looking in amazement at this tiny, semifurnished room! A crafting table, a furnace, even a bed, and, wouldn't you know it, carpet! White wool carpet I almost mistook for snow. And there were windows, too. Windows of ice that I'd missed from the outside because they must have been blocked by falling snow.

"What the . . ." I began, mind racing, as an outside growl pulled me back to reality.

"Right," I told the door. "I'll be with you in a minute." Gobbling down a few baked potatoes, I began to calculate how I'd be able to take down my three furry jailors.

They're already wounded, I reasoned as food put the hyper back in my hyper-healing, *so maybe just a swipe or two each . . . Maybe if I open the door and let one in at a time . . .*

"Yeeuuu!" A yelp from outside, a cry of canine pain.

I tried looking out the windows again. Damn snow.

Another squeal, right after a barely recognizable sound.

THWP! There it was again, the twang of a bow, the whistle of an arrow, and the unmistakable THUNK of it striking home.

"Yeeeuuu" came a third and final yelp. Then, nothing. Silence. Waiting.

"Hello?" A voice, not mine. Not in my head! A real, honest-to-goodness voice right outside! "Hello? Anyone in there?"

"No . . ." Lungs filling, heart drumrolling. "No, it can't . . ."

I threw open the door.

And there she was.

CHAPTER 5

"Well, I see you've found my hunting cabin."

Green eyes. Skin lighter than mine.

"Well, not technically mine, in the sense that I didn't build it myself. The thing just sort of popped into existence one day, like the rabbits and polar bears, and, well, I suppose, me, and you, if you're anything like me."

A high voice. Soft. And with an accent?

"Well, go on then, say something." Clad from head to toe in leather, with a slowly lowering bow. "If not a 'thank you,' then at least a 'hello' would suffice."

Real? I couldn't believe it. I'd been burned so often, gotten my hopes up too many times. Illusion? Hallucination? Or, maybe like I'd believed that first day on the island, a dream?

"Well, maybe you can't speak."

I tried. I couldn't. Dizzy, mind racing. Too much to process, to believe.

"Or maybe you don't understand what I'm saying. Or maybe"—lowering the weapon fully—"you're just too cold for words. Heaven knows I was when I woke up here."

Packing the bow away, hands free to remove the hide helmet and chest plate.

"Here."

Tossed at my feet, hovering above the snow. "It's not exactly a winter coat, but rabbit hide does keep one warmer than diamond." With the helmet and chest plate gone, I could see a head of sunset golden hair, painted on, just like mine, but continuing down to a ponytail on a green shirt.

"You don't have to accept it, or if you'd prefer to change inside the igloo . . ."

Swift motions, away with the sword, shield, and diamond armor. The rabbit fur WAS warmer, not by much, but offering just enough flexibility to keep my body's warmed air within. The feeling of it against my skin, the physical sensation of touch. That's what I think finally broke me out of my stupor. One final sense to back up my eyes and ears.

This was real.

"Th . . . thank you."

"So, you do talk?" The laugh, the first real music I'd heard in this world. "And you're quite welcome."

"Thank you," I said again. "Thank you!" To my rescuer, to the sky, to luck! "Thank you, thank you, thank you!"

I didn't plan to run to her. And in my ecstatic stupor, I completely forgot that this world wouldn't let you hug.

"Hang on there!" Retreating quickly, backing up with waving hands. "A little personal space if you don't mind!"

"I'm sorry," I stammered. "I just . . . I've been alone for so long . . . I haven't had a friend to talk to since . . ."

"Hang on!" And, in a cooling tone, "We're not friends. We've only just met."

"Yeah, I know, but . . ." I spluttered, "I mean, c'mon, we're both not from here. You just said so, right? We're both strangers. Which makes us—"

"Strangers." Another step back. "To each other, as well as to this world. In fact, I know this world a good deal better than I know you."

"Oh, c'mon!" I pouted. "You know what I mean."

"I do, and you're wrong."

You're wrong. No one had ever said that to me before. At least no one I could remember. I'm sure that back in my world, our world, someone must have told me I was wrong at least once or twice. But since I'd woken up here, I'd had only my animal pals for conversation, and their "moos" and "bahs" had been but an outward expression of my inner monologues. Now here, for the first time, was a dialogue, a conversation with another thinking, talking person, who had just told me that what I believed was wrong.

"But," I pressed, talking way before my brain had time to okay the words, "there's, like, two of us now! And we're the same, and . . ."

"You don't know that." A third step backward. "You don't know that we come from the same world or even the same part of the same world. You don't know anything about me other than I look similar to you, and just because you look similar to someone . . ."

". . . doesn't make them a friend," I finished, quoting a rule I'd come up with after almost being poisoned by the witch. "Rule twenty-five." I gave a resigned sigh.

"Pardon?"

"Nothing, sorry, I'll tell you later . . . if"—and suddenly my stomach knotted—"there is a later? I mean, if you don't want company or anything . . ."

"No, no, let's not be dramatic." A slight chuckle, and my insides began to relax. "I'm just saying you can't be friends with someone you don't know yet, and I don't know anything about you." A small, welcome step closer. "I don't even know your name."

"Oh, yeah." My turn to chuckle. "Right. I'm . . . I . . . totally don't know what my name is!"

"Really?" A loud laugh this time, warm and kind. "I was just winding you up! I don't know my name either! Never needed to. No one to address me up till now."

"Ha!" I guffawed back. "I know, right?! I guess we need names. I'll be—"

"No, no, let me name you." Leaning closer, again, examining me up and down. "So much more fun! Like that book about the lad who's shipwrecked on the island and names a native after a day of the week . . . although it probably should have been the other way around, don't you think? A bit twisted, him being the visitor and casting himself as lord?"

I just shrugged. I'd heard of the book, and, full disclosure, if I'd ever bothered to read it, it might have made my real-life island trial a heck of a lot easier.

One more thing I gotta do when I get home.

"So, let's see what we can see . . ." Green eyes continued to look me over. "We'll, you're a guy . . ."

"I am?" I asked, genuinely surprised. "How do you know?"

"Well, you have a beard."

"I do?!"

"Definitely. A little brown, goatee thingy round your mouth."

"Really." After all this time, all of my amazing accomplishments and discoveries, I still hadn't figured out a way to see my own reflection. "I guess, if I really think about it, I have kinda always thought of myself as a guy."

"'Guy,'" she repeated. "About as proper as anything else."

"And you," I began.

"Well, I'm definitely a girl."

"Really?" Okay, for the record, while I've been referring to her as a girl in these pages, and while I'd been thinking of her as a girl, I, until this moment, had no actual evidence to do that. I mean, dudes can have long hair, and a high voice doesn't mean anything. In fact, I wasn't even sure that she had a high voice, because of her accent, which seemed to lilt musically when she spoke.

"How do you know you're a girl?" I asked.

"It's how I feel and it's the type of name I want."

"Fair enough," I answered. "Do you want me to call you Girl?"

"Oh good Lord, no!" she exclaimed. "Do you always name

things so literally?" Before I could point out that she'd just named me "Guy," she continued, "It's got to be something thoughtful, something powerful and strong and beautiful that I don't mind hearing at any random moment during the day."

"Oh, is that all?" I asked sarcastically. "No pressure there." And she laughed again, that wonderful laugh that warmed me like a summer breeze.

"Summer," I said confidently. Then, "I mean, if that's cool with you."

She took a moment, mentally digesting it, then nodded. "Perfect."

I think a lot of cultures on my world have a lot of different greetings. I think some shake hands, some bow, some put their hands over their hearts. That one's my favorite, but, like almost all the other gestures, is impossible for my rigid, angular form to accomplish. What I could do, and did, was step within arm's length and extend the soft flesh cube of my hand.

"Nice to meet you, Summer."

She copied my motion exactly, bumping my fist with hers. "Nice to meet you, Guy."

I'd like to say it was the touch of her fist, the solid, reassuring human contact that made me shiver. But, in all honesty, I was probably just cold.

"Ggghghgh." I shivered, which produced a giggling response from Summer.

"Come on then," she said, turning away. "Let's get you home and properly warmed up."

"Home?" I asked, noticing that she'd turned away from the igloo. "Isn't this where you live?"

"Are you mad?" she asked as she walked away.

"Well," I said, running to keep up, "didn't you say it appeared when you did?"

"Oh, if only," she answered, leading me back in the general direction of the coast. "This just recently came along, long after I really needed it. When I first got here . . ."

She began at her beginning, and wow did I try to listen to every word. But it was so hard with my mind racing through everything that was happening.

I wasn't alone anymore! I'd found . . . well, not a friend—Summer seemed pretty clear about that. But why? Why the distance? Why wasn't she just as happy to find me as I was to find her? I figured I'd ask her later, after I'd earned her friendship.

This was a new type of lesson, a friendship-lesson, or what I'd like to call a "fresson." I know, I know—me, always having to figure out the rules. But it'd been the key to my survival all this time. Crafting, mining, monsters: Everything has rules, and as my own lesson number seven states, "Figuring out the rules turns them from enemies into friends."

It made sense that it couldn't be any different with friendship. There had to be boundaries, rights and wrongs. Especially when dealing with another human being. This would be way more complicated, and potentially more hazardous, than dealing with my simple animal pals. Just thinking about all the ways to mess up made me shiver more than the cold did. I couldn't afford to alienate her or drive her away and ruin my one chance to not be alone again.

I realized I'd have to learn a whole long list of fressons, with the second one right on the heels of the first.

Friends listen.

So I did, fighting through all the inner thoughts you've just read to try to pay attention to what she was talking about. I know I missed more than a few details (and fortunately she didn't quiz me later), but I got the basic gist of her origin.

Like me, Summer'd woken up underwater, shot for the surface, found herself alone, and swum until she'd sighted land.

Unlike me, however, she wasn't lucky enough to find a lush green island. She'd come ashore on the ice-crusted beach. No apple trees, no animal companions. She'd begun starving on day one, and had that been me, I'm pretty sure I wouldn't have lived past day two.

She'd taken out a lone spruce tree within minutes of walking ashore and discovered how to make a crafting table immediately, and from there how to make tools and weapons. If you read my first book, you know how long that took me, and how long it also took me to get up the courage to fight my first monster. Summer didn't have that luxury.

That first night on the ice, as the sun set and the mobs rose, she'd had to fight for her life with a wooden axe and sword until she'd killed enough zombies (or "zeds" as she called them) to live on their flesh for days. Because that's what she did, and without any cow milk to chase away the hyper-hunger.

Those first few days were brutal: freezing, exploring, constantly sick and hungry from barely enough toxic ghoul meat to survive. She couldn't fish, because she didn't know about spider silk yet. And she couldn't hunt rabbits because, back then, there hadn't been any. Apparently, this "taiga" (her word) had originally been emptier than when I'd arrived.

I honestly don't think I would have made it, especially given how long it took me to start figuring things out. I probably would have just wasted away in some hand-dug hole. It'd almost happened my first night on the island, burying myself alive as a zombie lurked outside. Had that happened here, and if I'd been as hungry, cold, and injured as Summer, I might have just given up.

She never did. She always fought back. And those early wins, both on the battlefield and on the crafting table, had given her the confidence to keep moving. Down the coast and then inland, looking for, well, something better, including a chance for rescue. That'd sure been my goal, when I'd first reached the island. But because it was an island, I'd been forced to stay in one place and make do with what I had. With her, there had always been the hope of something beyond the next ridge.

I think the term is "nomadic," although she described it as being a "hunter-gatherer." She'd gathered crafting wood from trees by day and hunted zombies for their flesh by night. She hadn't thought of mining yet, or agriculture. Those had had to come with staying put.

Which came with the discovery of the cave.

It was on the morning of the tenth day (can you believe it— ten whole days?!) that she'd climbed up the bank of a frozen river and saw what looked like a dark hole at the base of a lonely mountain. She hadn't thought of investigating, but when a zombie shambled out and promptly burned into that morning's breakfast, her hunter's instincts thought there might be more inside. While there weren't, she did discover something just as valuable as food: shelter.

After so much fruitless wandering, Summer had realized it might be a good time to stop and figure out a new strategy. And this cave seemed like a safe enough place to do it. Especially after exploring the shallow interior and finding the same blessed game changer that had chased my nightmares away: coal! With torches fixed to the wall, and a door she'd previously—and accidentally—crafted against the entrance, she finally had a safe space to think, experiment, and grow.

Agriculture, iron—you get it. One advance after another, including advances into the cave itself, which, apparently, I'd walked right over and past without ever realizing it. Because just as Summer finished telling me what I've just told you, she stopped at the base of—get this!—the volcano!

CHAPTER 6

"You live here?" Standing there like a dweeb, I stared at the very thing I'd first run to, then discounted, then explored (I thought), and finally left way behind me. "Here?"

"Why the surprise?" asked Summer. "Haven't you been listening to my story?"

"Oh, yeah, sure," I backpedaled, "but I'd been here, like, just this morning, and I didn't, like, see a cave or anything."

"You weren't supposed to," she said matter-of-factly, then started up the very same lava slope. Had I missed a door somewhere? A hatch?

"Here we are," she announced, stopping at that lone red flower. Then, reaching over it, she plucked out a cube of dirt to reveal a shallow recess behind it. Peering inside, I saw a standard wood and stone lever fixed to the floor.

"Go on then," she said, inching out of the way, "you do the honors."

Without moving, I used this world's four-block extended reach.

The lever flicked forward, with the compound noise of something else behind it. I thought I'd heard that sound before, that mysterious CLICK when I'd been exploring the mountain. Whatever those had been, this one definitely stopped the flow of lava.

"Just give it a moment," said Summer, replacing the camouflaging earth cube before leading me back down the slope. "It takes a bit, but well worth the wait."

And it was! I gasped as the last bits of molten rock dropped away to reveal a four-by-four block recess that ended in double doors. "A secret entrance!" I cooed. "So cool!"

"Oh, this is nothing," she said, leading me through the dark spruce doors. Warm, welcoming air embraced me. And not just warm. Wet, or, at least it felt that way compared with the ice-desert atmosphere I'd been breathing.

I could see a long, torchlit hallway beyond, and as Summer stepped inside, I thought I heard another CLICK. I should have just followed her in, instead of stopping at the threshold to investigate.

"OW!" I yelped as the door promptly slammed on my face.

"Mind the pressure plates," she said, reopening the door with a giggle. "They keep the mobs out and hot air in. At least they used to before I put in my lava upgrade."

"Good to know," I grumbled, stepping over the clicking, mini-cube-thick panels.

"I suppose you don't have to worry too much about weather where you spawned."

"Not much," I answered, "I came ashore at—"

"Just a moment," she interrupted, then led me down a narrow side passage. "Can't forget to set everything right." I could see her reaching up into a hole in the ceiling, about where I judged the lava lever to be.

TH-CHCK. That same noise from before, machinery moving above my head, along with a faint bubbling that had to be the boiling rock.

"Now," continued Summer. "Let's get you properly warmed."

She led me back down the main hallway to a single, mercifully non-pressure-plate door. And beyond that door was the closest thing I'd seen in this world to a luxury hotel suite.

I guess I was expecting something like my bunker: smooth stone walls, a crafting table, maybe a furnace or two, and the obligatory double and single storage chests. They were all there, all right, but everything around them . . .

A fully carpeted floor, striped red and yellow, and dark spruce planks for walls. And nearly every square of wall was covered with what I recognized as item frames. I'd read about them in one of the manuals but could never construct them because a primary ingredient was animal hide.

Clearly Summer didn't have that problem (neither with the supply or, I would later confirm, the morality). I counted twenty-one in total, each holding a different make and model of this world's tools. Axe, pick, shovel, and hoe, from plain wood right up to glittering diamond.

And the final frame held a golden disk. It was similar to a compass, but instead of a needle, this face held the picture of day slowly rotating into night.

"Is that a clock?" I asked, thinking I might have seen its design in one of the manuals.

"Don't you have one?" asked Summer.

"Never needed one." I shrugged. "I lived aboveground on an island. The sun was the only clock I needed."

"Well, I didn't have that luxury at first," Summer explained, with just the slightest hint of defensiveness. "The first few weeks, I gambled with my life every time I opened the door."

The thought made me shudder. To not know if it was day or night outside? Mobs aside, just being cut off from the natural world must have been a brutal experience. It sounded like torture to be locked in a room with no windows and either darkness or the light of torches all the time. It sounded like it would really mess with your head, break down your spirit. Those first few weeks for Summer, with the constant cold and a starvation diet of zombie flesh . . .

"How'd you do it?" I asked, realizing that I'd heard only the first part of her story. "Once you found this place, how'd you turn things around?"

"I dug." Summer looked up to a mounted stone pickaxe. "The coal gave me an incentive to keep going, to see what else I could find underground. I tunneled and explored and found all the usual minerals and such. But when I discovered the abandoned mineshaft . . ."

"Hey! Me too!" I blurted, excited at this connecting coincidence. "Did you find some cool stuff?"

"If by 'cool stuff,'" Summer continued, "you mean the means to survive without ever having to go topside again."

To me, the idea seemed crazy. Underground all day every day? Never seeing the sun or feeling the wind on your face? "Really?" was all I could ask.

"Really," she answered quickly, but sensing my follow-up question, added, "Of course, I obviously did, but only after discovering the books that told me how to make this."

She gestured to the clock.

"And, a few weeks later, these." Her eyes fell on something below the clock, a line of glass blocks I'd mistook for the gravel behind them.

"How about a little natural light?" she asked, and flicked a floor lever I'd also missed.

"Just like the lava," she boasted. "Pistons and levers and a line of that marvelous redstone."

I was about to jump in with stories of my own "marvelous" redstone inventions, how I'd used them to make awesome mine-clearing booby traps, but the thoughts never made their way into spoken words, as my eyes caught something odd about the position of the windows. They looked right out onto the path I'd used to climb the mountain. Right about where I'd heard that clicking noise the first time I'd been here.

"Summer," I asked, a little hesitantly, "earlier, when I was climbing your mountain, I heard that same sound, and, well, I thought it was a rabbit that killed itself."

"Oh, they are rather daft," Summer chuckled. "Those poor little fuzzies."

"Yeah," I said, unsure of how to proceed, "but that's not the point." I suddenly felt my stomach tense, my jaw tighten. I couldn't understand why I was suddenly so nervous, until the words had actually left my mouth. "Did you . . . like . . . see me? Out there?"

A pause. Summer's eyes locked on me.

"No." Flat, unemotional. Then, "I might have opened the windows. I do that in the morning to check if the coast is clear." Another beat, barely a second for breath. "But I didn't see you." And suddenly, "You don't have the rabbit, do you?"

"Wha?" I started to ask, a little confused at the abrupt change of subject.

"The hopper." She pressed. "You said it leapt to its death right in front of you."

"Yeah." I nodded, rummaging. "Yeah, I still got the body somewhere in my . . ."

"How about I cook it for you?" she asked cheerily. "Whip up a nice hot rabbit stew while you shower."

The words came out as one. "Ohthanksyeahthat'dbe SHOWER?!"

"A steam shower," she chimed. "Best way to chase away the chills." She pointed to something behind me, another single door in the wall. "There's a frame in the washroom if you'd like to hang your armor."

I wasn't sure what to say other than, "Um, thank you."

"Don't mention it," she said happily. "Just hand over the hopper."

I tossed her the little pink carcass, which she grabbed before turning back to the crafting table. "Well, go on—it'll only take a minute. I've got the ingredients in my kit."

The door opened to a whoosh of hot, humid air.

"Don't let all the steam out," she said, closing the door behind me.

I found myself in a polished gray bathroom that put the model in my first house to shame. There was an armor frame, a storage chest, a raised "toilet" with its water hemmed in by stairs. There was also a "sink," I judged, by the wall cube gushing out into another raised hole. Exactly what you'd need for washing your hands after using the toilet, which as I knew by then was impossible on both counts.

I remember, at that moment, having felt strangely validated that this other human had also built a useless, decorative monument to that other life, but those musings quickly vanished when I turned to the side.

Just as with the toilet, Summer had learned to craft a HOT TUB! Water above glass above lava. "Aw yeah!" I sang, doing my signature happy dance. "Hot tubbin'," I crooned, spinning and hopping and throwing my armor on the frame, "hot tubbin' time!"

That feeling! Those first delicious seconds of skin sinking into scalding water. "Wh-ugh," I groaned, and I shook as the heat leapt up my legs, through my spine, literally expelling the frosty tension from my body. I thought I'd appreciated the sensation on my temperate island. But here, after a day and a night of freezing, of chattering, stabbingly cruel cold, it was perfect.

I groaned again, eyes closed, feeling every muscle in my body start to unwind.

"You all right in there?" asked Summer through the door.

"Wha . . . oh . . . yeah!" I answered, standing embarrassedly still. Now that there was another pair of ears around, that whole talking-to-myself thing would have to go!

"I thought you might actually be a different life-form that needed to use the toilet."

"Oh, no," I laughed, "just enjoying the tub!"

Well, that's one question answered.

"Have you tried the shower yet?"

I'd forgotten, too engrossed in the steamy goodness of the tub. "Not yet."

"Just above your head," she called.

Right in front of me and one block above was another of her mysterious levers, and directly above my head was a shallow hole in the ceiling.

"Got it," I called back, reaching for the lever. "Thanks."

FFFFT!

Water. Hot water! Falling all around me, encasing my face in a column of blissful blue.

I started to laugh at the joy I felt at this wonderful invention, but instead gurgled, forgetting I was now underwater. I'd forgotten how much I hated to be underwater. "Ooouuugh," I choked.

I couldn't stay submerged forever. Unlike in my world, showering meant holding your breath. But those few, glorious seconds replaced every hour of frosty torture.

Summer was right. It was the only proper way to warm up.

What an amazing way to use a piston, I thought, relishing the scalding rain. *Just like the windows and the lava.*

Windows and lava.

Why?

The question rose like steam. *Why is she using gravel to hide her windows, and lava to hide her doors? In fact . . .*

A bigger question behind the first.

Why is she trying to hide at all? Why not announce her presence to the world? Like I did with my first "HELP" sign on the hill?

Another dunk under the shower, another layer of mental mystery.

Maybe she gave up on being rescued. I did, after a while, but if someone had come along, they would have seen my house, and certainly my observation tower. I didn't try to hide from anything, or . . . anyone?

And what was that pause when I asked her about seeing me? *Was she telling the . . .*

"Supper's on" came a muffled call.

"Be right there," I bubbled, and hopped out of the tub to dress. I suddenly felt guilty for questioning Summer's motives. There had to be a reasonable explanation.

Maybe she has to hide, I thought, slipping my armor back on. *This land's a lot bigger than my safe little island, and if there are other, smarter monsters here that could track her down . . .*

I switched off the shower, opened the washroom door, and walked out to Summer's presenting a bowl of steaming, aromatic stew.

"A bit uncivilized," she said, tossing the bowl at my feet, "but well worth it in the end, don't you think?"

I did, even if the experience was slightly forced for Summer's benefit. No, I didn't eat animals, but this one had died by accident, and I didn't want to be rude to my host. I figured just this once would be okay, and later I could explain my dietary beliefs.

And, yeah, I might as well come clean: It was SO delicious. Gobbling down every delectable morsel almost made me regret my life choice not to hunt. "Mm-mmm-mmmm," I moaned, producing a lyrical laugh from the chef.

"It can't be all that," she said with a hint of embarrassment.

"It is!" I moaned. "With, what, potato, carrot, and mushroom! You actually made mushrooms taste good."

"Don't knock mushrooms," she warned playfully. "They were my first step up from zed guts."

"Why do you call them 'zeds'?" I asked. "Why not zombies?"

"Just seemed quicker," she said with a shrug, "to use the last letter in the alphabet."

"That's a Z," I corrected, making sure to pronounce it "zee."

"I'm afraid that's a zed," she counter-corrected, which confirmed that we might be speaking two versions of the same language.

"We gotta be from different parts of our world," I said.

"Or," she suggested, "different worlds that both need a toilet."

I started to laugh, but it came out as a long, unexpected yawn.

"Sorry," I said, still yawning. "Been a long day."

Summer nodded, glancing at the darkening sky beyond her windows. "Let's get you bedded down for the night." Flicking the window lever shut, she took back my empty, clean bowl (how cool is it that this world doesn't make you have to wash dishes?!). Then, opening another door opposite the bathroom, she led me into another cozy, well-furnished bedroom. Gray and blue checkered carpet, wood-paneled walls, paintings on the wall (the same ones I had in my house!), and an embedded, brick-built, three-block-wide column against the far wall. I was going to ask what this unfamiliar construction was for, but first things first.

"Where should I set up my bed?" I asked, mentally measuring each section of open floor.

"Eh?" Summer sounded confused, then motioned to the single bed opposite the column. "This *is* your bed."

Now my confusion. "But where will you sleep?"

"Ah!" Summer laughed at a joke I was yet to be let in on. "This isn't my room! I'll be just down the hall, in the main chamber."

"Main chamber," I repeated, wrapping my brain around the term. "You mean this isn't . . ."

"No, no, no," she giggled. "Not for ages. It's more like my vestibule now, or, I guess, my guest room."

There was more? More rooms under this mountain? More wonders? More crazy cool stuff to see?

"Can I see the main chamber now?" I asked, as fatigue brought up another, contradicting yawn.

"Tomorrow," she said, walking over to a hole in the brick column. "You can leave the washroom door open if you'd like. The shower should keep you warm enough. Or . . ."

Producing a flint and steel, she threw a spark into the hole.

Flames blazed to life.

A fireplace!

"I love going to sleep by its light," she said, stepping back next to me. "Even though it can get a bit whiffy."

That smell.

Just like when I'd been climbing the slope!

That hole I'd found must have been the outlet of a chimney, and the eggy, sulfurous smell must have come from this, or maybe another, fireplace.

"I used to use wood," she explained, "but it doesn't burn indefinitely like netherrack."

A new word.

"Netherrack?"

"You don't have any?" Now Summer sounded really confused. "You've never been to the Nether?"

"What's . . . Where's the Nether?"

"Tomorrow," she repeated soothingly, then headed past me for the door. "We'll talk over breakfast tomorrow."

"Uh, thanks," I stammered at her back. "Thanks for dinner and the shower, and, you know, everything."

Summer turned to face me. "You're welcome, Guy." Then headed out with, "Sleep well."

"Um, you too . . ." I called to the closed door, as a new type of warmth, the warmth of a single word settled on me.

Welcome.

I'm welcome.

I know it's just something people are supposed to say, but here, now . . .

Summer had welcomed me into her home, into her life. Maybe she wasn't ready to call me a friend yet, but there'd be time enough for that. The point was that all the big challenges were now behind me. No more having to struggle, to figure everything out, to feel like it was always me alone against the whole world.

Body warmed and belly full, I slipped between the soft, comforting blankets of my bed, staring at the "whiffy" fire as sleep wrapped me in protective arms.

"I'm not alone anymore," I yawned, closing my eyes. "I'm not alone."

CHAPTER 7

The next morning, I woke to the smell of . . . well, you know. But I didn't care. Summer was right about getting used to the fireplace. And besides, there was so much wonderfulness to wake up to: the crackling fire, the flicker it cast on the wood walls, the memories of yesterday, and the anticipation of seeing the rest of Summer's mountain today.

I sprang out of bed with the speed of a dog about to go for a walk. I threw on my armor, opened my guest room door, and trotted down the hallway to the double doors. There was no way I could have imagined anything close to what my eyes took in the moment those dark wood partitions parted.

"Whoa."

How do I describe that underground palace? How do I even begin?

I guess it makes sense to just start at the sheer size of the hollowed-out room (because I learned later that Summer had, in fact, picked it out from solid rock!). Two dozen blocks—twenty-four!—across and high! A quarter, or maybe a third of the entire mountain was this one single cavern.

And at its center was another hot tub! No, hot *pool*! At least three times as large, and surrounded on all sides by irrigated rows of crops. Wheat, carrots, potatoes, watermelons, pumpkins, and some other root crop I didn't recognize at first, but that Summer told me later were beets. And behind them, on the four corners of this indoor farm, trees! Oak trees!

I didn't kill the last ones! I thought, feeling suddenly absolved of the eco disaster I'd committed on my island. And this beautiful, impossible grove, growing tall and healthy by nothing more than torchlight, was just the beginning of what continued to take my breath away.

Hundreds of torches lined the smooth, gray stone walls, broken by at least a dozen doors per floor. That's right, there were *two* floors. This room had two stories to it, the second one ringed by a railed, wraparound oak balcony.

How to get up there? There wasn't any staircase or ladder.

I called "Summer!" but didn't get a response. She had to be behind one of those doors, maybe sleeping or having breakfast.

Will this world let me knock? What if I barged in on her in the middle of a steam shower?

Steam shower.

The thought almost sent me back to my guest room for a quick, heavenly soak. But why bother when this Olympic-sized pool was right in front of me.

It looked so inviting, so absolutely decadent. If only I could dive in from way up on the balcony. But for right now, a running jump would have to do.

She won't mind, I reasoned, backing up a few steps. *A quick dip should give her more time to finish whatever she's doing.* I took a deep breath, lined up my leap, then sprinted forward.

"STOP!"

Summer's voice, freezing me in place like in a cartoon. One more advantage to the whacked-out physics of this world: no momentum.

Stone still, my feet barely a mini-cube from the edge, I looked up to see Summer calling down from the railing. "Bad idea."

Looking down, I saw why. The pool's bottom wasn't standard glass-covered lava. This surface had dark brownish splotches within brighter, glowing veins that shifted from dull yellow to muted orange. And above it all, the water. Not just steaming, but literally boiling, a pond of angry bubbles popping right below my face.

"Magma blocks," said Summer. "Very common down in the Nether."

There was that word again: Nether.

"Be right down," she called, and disappeared behind one of the upper doors.

Three seconds later she was bounding out one of the lower doors toward me. "The boiling water does wonders to humidify the air, but you wouldn't want to walk on them, trust me. And walking is all you can do, because the bubbles won't let you swim."

She glanced past me at what was essentially a giant cooking pot. "Can't imagine a more dreadful way to go."

I was about to ask her about the Nether, this mysterious place of "magma blocks" and "netherrack," when her eyes darted past me again, up this time, to a clock on the far wall.

"You're just in time." And trotting past me to another door, she added, "Fancy a leg of mutton?"

"Mutton?" Another new word.

"I know," she chuckled, "it sounds a little heavy for breakfast, but I think I remember having sheep for breakfast occasionally."

Sheep?

Uh-oh.

"Yeah, well . . ." I hemmed, feeling a nervous sweat break out above my eyes.

Yes, I'd eaten the rabbit stew last night, and yes, I'd saved wolf-killed sheep meat in my pack for emergencies. But this wasn't an emergency, and, honestly, even if it had been, could I eat something I'd just come to consider a friend?

Okay, judge if you want to. I guess if you're into absolutes this does sound a little wishy-washy. But, at least for me, eating a rabbit that I'd never bonded with seemed a world apart from eating a sheep I'd fed, talked to, and had actually risked my own life to protect.

I couldn't do it. But could I refuse her generosity?

"I'm sorry I don't have any on hand," Summer continued, "which is why I was out hunting when we met."

Hunting?! She wanted me to go hunting?! For sheep?!

"Here we go." I watched her pull four bushels of wheat from a chest. "To replenish the members of the flock we take."

Think fast! Redirect!

"No need," I stammered, fumbling for the remains in my pack. "I've totally got some mutton if you want it."

"Oh brill," Summer chirped as I handed her the meat-wrapped bones. "Thank you, Guy."

One bullet dodged. One to go.

"And," I nodded, grasping at what she'd just said, "ya know, you're right about mutton so early in the morning for me." Bingo!

Just tell her you don't eat meat, I told myself as she led me into her spacious, ornate kitchen. My internal wrestling faded away at the sight of brick walls, oak floors, ceiling beams made from the trunks of trees that were as unfamiliar as the brown, pod-looking things attached to them. What was familiar were the cakes, several of them, sitting ever-fresh on half-plank shelves between storage chests.

"Won't be a minute," she said, and slid the sheep limb into one of the furnaces.

As the flames instantly lit and the room filled with undeniably tempting smells, she asked, "And what can I get for you?"

"Oh, I'm fine," I said, trying to play it cool. "I'm really not that hungry."

GRRRP, growled my traitorous stomach.

Two against one!

"You must have something," insisted Summer. "A baked potato, a loaf of bread, or . . ."

Reaching back into the chest, she produced a roundish red treasure. "Care for an—"

"Yes, please!"

An apple! How long had it been? How many days, how many meals, how many times had I missed that juicy sweetness?

"Mm . . . mmm . . . mmmm!" I crunched on the delicious treat.

"Would you like a moment alone?" Summer asked, giggling at her own joke. I was barely listening. As the taste ran down my throat, it brought up more feelings than I could handle. That first comforting apple on that first, terrifying day. The desperation of burning the seedlings for fuel, the despair and guilt at knowing that I'd destroyed an entire food supply. The wondering if any more apple-bearing oak trees lay anywhere beyond the horizon. And now, this second chance, this brighter future. This snack of hope!

"More?" I groaned, and without asking, without thinking, I pushed past Summer and reached for the open chest.

The lid slammed, and suddenly Summer's face was right in front of mine. "Oi!" She barked. "Didn't anyone ever tell you it's not polite to grab?"

"Sorry," I said, snapping out of my euphoria.

Fresson three: Friends respect each other's property.

"I didn't mean to grab," I explained. "I just haven't seen one in a long time."

"It's all right," said Summer, her voice calming to an even pitch. "Just please ask next time before you go snooping."

"Deal," I replied, hoping that was the end of it, and it was, because then she opened the chest again and said, "Well, if you're still hungry . . ."

What she tossed me next was roundish again, but flat, and brown like bread with darker brown flecks that looked exactly like they smelled.

"Fancy a biscuit?"

I did, but that sure wasn't a biscuit where I come from. Back in my part of the other world, I'm pretty sure a biscuit was a light, fluffy, salty muffin thing you had with fried chicken. And that wasn't what she tossed me now.

Sweet and chewy, and filled with gooey nuggets.

A cookie! An honest-to-goodness chocolate chip cookie!

"How?!" was all I could say, savoring every bite.

"Easy," shrugged Summer, her face rising to the beams above my head, "once you get your hands on some cocoa beans."

So that's what those pod-looking things were!

"You have chocolate!" I gasped, and quickly repeated, "How?"

"Farther to the west"—Summer pointed to the wall—"past the forest, and the next tundra, there's a deep jungle. Massive trees. Tall as mountains. With cocoa pods growing on some of them."

She reached up, swiped at one of the hanging pods, and caught a collection of brown beans. "They only grow on this type of jungle wood, though," she explained, refastening some beans back up to the beam, which immediately morphed into a small, light green pod. "I'll have to take you there sometime," she added, handing me another cookie and taking one for herself.

"You bet!" I answered, raising my confection to toast hers. "Maybe we'll make some time to explore it when passing through."

"Passing through?" Summer suddenly lowered her biscuit.

"Yeah," I answered before crunching down on the cookie. "You know, when we get going."

Now the cookie was back in her belt. "Going where?"

"Well," I began, with growing confusion, "anywhere. Anywhere there's answers."

"Answers?"

I suddenly realized that Summer had no idea what I was talking about. And why should she? In the short time we'd known each other, I'd learned a lot more about her story than the other way around.

"Sorry," I began, "you don't know my story. I guess we haven't had time yet. Well, it all started—"

"Tell me while we work," Summer cut me off. "This morning's crops need harvesting."

Which we did, heading into the garden, collecting any ripe wheat, carrots, potatoes, and beets. And in the process, I filled her in on everything I'd been through up until that point. I told her about the island, my challenges and triumphs. And she was a pretty good listener, nodding and "mm-ing" as we gathered her garden's bounty. Every so often she'd cut in with a question about something I'd done, or a lighthearted, even teasing comment like "Another lesson?" or "It took you that long to figure that bit out?" Again, it was all in fun. Until the story changed to why I left the island.

Okay, at the time, I wondered if it was all in my head, as we took the crops back into the kitchen and organized them into different storage chests. But I could swear that her teasing barbs and listening "mm's" faded to practically nothing. And when I finally wrapped up my story with "So you see, I came here to answer all the really big questions about this world, and, hopefully, find a way to return to my world . . . our world. Right?" Summer just looked at me blankly. That was the moment I realized one of the biggest disadvantages about this blocky, limited form: You can't read someone's face!

I'd never thought about it until then, never had any reason to. But now, with another person right in front of me, I realized that there's a whole language of expression that goes far beyond spoken words.

A smile, a frown, even a raised eyebrow. So many ways to complement your speech, or react to someone else's. I'd never considered that when someone is listening to me, they're speaking volumes before they even open their mouth. Now it was all gone, and I was staring into a face so flat and unresponsive it was as if I was, literally, talking to a wall.

All except the eyes. At least she told me something with those. But what? What did glancing at the floor mean?

"You wan'em too, right?" I blathered on, my confusion rising. "You wanna answer those same questions and, of course, you wanna get home."

"Yes," Summer finally answered after what might have been the briefest of pauses, "yes, of course I'd love to find my way home, I just"—again, a beat—"I haven't had much time, what with trying to survive and learning new skills."

"Yeah," I said, interrupting with a wash of relief, "totally. I was the same way. And maybe if I'd had more land to explore, I might have stayed closer to home, I mean my house, I mean . . . You get it. Point is, now that there are two of us . . ."

"Yes, most definitely." Now it was Summer's turn to interrupt. "And we will, definitely. We'll set off for the great unknown soon enough." Another half-beat. "But not yet." And then, more confidently. "Not until I'm finished."

"Hm?" I wonder what expression my round, soft face would have made at that.

"I'm working on something," she said, heading for the kitchen's back door. "Here, let me show you what I mean."

I suddenly felt a slight queasiness, and it didn't have to do with eating too many cookies. What was going on with Summer? Why the pauses, the hesitation in her voice? Why wasn't she jumping at the chance to help me find our way home? Was it tied to her weirdness with the windows?

I figured I'd find out soon enough as we passed through the back door into her workshop. It was actually more like a factory, with walls of furnaces, a dozen double chests, two anvils, two crafting tables, and a pillar of lava encased in glass. "My washroom tub's right above it," she explained, sensing what had to be my coming question. "You'll see."

We passed through another door, up a flight of stone steps, and into a palatial bathroom that made my little guest room model look like a cheap motel. All the amenities but twice the size and built from a polished pink stone I'd thought useless until that moment.

"If your feet feel warm," she said over her shoulder, "that's the magma blocks under the floor." I stopped for a second, just long enough to feel the warmth through my shoes.

"Best feeling, first thing in the morning." Summer continued talking as she opened another pair of doors. "This is what I mean by 'unfinished.' This is where I sleep."

At first, I couldn't see anything. The room was pitch dark. Then . . .

Flick!

The luxury! Solid purple carpet, pinkish jungle wood walls. Paintings and framed maps and a clock fixed to the dormant, double-wide fireplace opposite a double bed between a disc player on one side and a potted blue flower on the other. And all of it illuminated by a glowing ceiling of dark yellow cubes.

"Redstone lamps," said Summer, "all wired together by redstone trails."

"Wha . . ." I could barely whisper. "How . . ."

"Have a go," she said, stepping back from the lever.

I reached out to switch it off.

Darkness.

Flick!

Light.

Flick-flick-flick.

Disco.

"How did you . . ." I began.

"Here." Summer opened a side door to a storage closet lit by another lamp. "Just redstone and glowstone," she said, opening a chest to toss me the wondrous cube. "Four, then four, nothing more."

Nothing more?!

It was unbelievable, that amazing little device in my hand. The ability to turn night into day. The power, the control. I still remember the rush of lighting my first torch, of never having to be afraid of the dark. But these torches never went out and, even though it never bothered me much to sleep with the lights on, I hadn't imagined I could re-create the light switches of my home world. And with nothing more than redstone and . . .

"Glowstone?"

"You've never seen glowstone?" Summer sounded puzzled.

I shook my head.

"Not even from a witch?"

Another shake. How many witches had she killed?

"It took a while," Summer elaborated, "to gather enough glowstone to make my first block. And I thought that was something, the fact that it glowed forever. But when I found that redstone book with all its recipes . . ."

I had that same book, I think, unless there were different versions around. Had I missed the part about lamps?

"In fact," Summer continued, "the one you're holding is the first one I ever made. Back before I discovered the Nether."

Again with that word.

"What is that?" I asked. "The Nether you keep mentioning."

"You really don't know." More a statement than a question. "You really must have been isolated on that little island."

"What's the Nether?" I pressed.

"A whole other world," said Summer, "or, perhaps, a part of this world you can only reach by a portal."

"A portal?!" How often had I dreamed of finding those? "You found a portal?"

"Made," said Summer, and, with calming, knowing hands raised, added, "and it can't get us home."

I sighed in response, trying to get past my disappointment.

"I found a book in one of the abandoned mineshafts that explains everything: how to make a portal to the Nether, what kind of mobs lurk there, what treasures you can find, including more glowstone than an army of witches could cough up." She gestured to the ceiling. "That's how I gathered enough to light this room, and"—she walked over to another set of double doors, threw them open, and swept her stubby, angled arm over the expanse of the main chamber—"eventually the entire mountain."

And then I understood, even before she spoke. "You see, once I start on a project, I can't just abandon it. I've worked too hard on this mountain, and all that's left is to light up the rest of the chambers. Once I do that, there'll be nothing left to do."

"That makes sense," I nodded.

And it really did. How many projects had I started that took up all my attention and time? Would I have just dropped the building of my house, or the torch-lighting of my island, if someone had come along and asked me to leave? Maybe, maybe not. I will say that even when I eventually decided to leave the island, I'd spent days getting everything in order for another traveler who might arrive after I'd gone. How cool would it be to leave a whole electrified mountain for someone to find?

It was such a relief to finally have such an uncomfortable mystery solved, and on the heels of that good feeling came an offer. "How about I help you? I can go to the Nether with you, help you collect more glowstone for these lamps?"

"Are you sure?" Summer looked back at the expansive ceiling before us. "I can't be sure how long that would take."

"It won't take as long if we do it together. And besides, it ain't like I'm going anywhere without you." I stepped closer, offering my fist. "How 'bout it?"

"Yes," answered Summer, "that would be lovely." Had she

hesitated just a half-breath before answering, or had it been my imagination? "Promise?" she asked, her hand still at her side. "Promise you won't go anywhere till we're done?"

"Promise," I said, fist still hovering.

Fresson four: Friends keep their promises.

"Right then." Her arm raised to bump. "Tomorrow, we journey to the Nether!"

CHAPTER 8

"Tomorrow?" I was raring to go. "Why not today, right now?"

"You can't just rush off to the Nether," balked Summer. "You need to prepare first."

"Oh, right," I nodded, and muttered to myself, "the Way of the Cube." This got me another blank-faced response.

"It's my method," I explained, "how I accomplish tasks. There are six points. Plan: What am I going to do? Prepare: How am I—"

"Yes, yes," Summer interjected, "I'm sure it's all a lovely list of witty wisdom, and I'd love to hear about it later, once we've gotten to work."

I was a little stunned, and yes, even a little hurt. It was one thing to have my animal pals walk away mid-sentence, but to be shushed by another human being was new.

"Well," I struggled, "sure, I guess, we can do it your way."

"If by 'way' you mean just doing what has to be done until it's all done without overthinking everything to death."

"Is that what you think I do?" It was a new feeling, being judged by another person. "You think I overthink everything to death?"

I must have sounded as hurt as I felt, because Summer clearly chose her next words. "Not that there's anything wrong with that," she said in a clearly mollifying tone. "We just have different methods that will have to be respected."

"I can't really argue with that," I agreed. "In fact, I think you coined a whole new fresson!"

"Fresson?" Summer asked warily, probably fearing what I'd say next.

"Friend lesson!" I proclaimed. "Even though we're not friends yet . . . I respected that, see? They're really an extension of all the personal lessons I've been compiling that I'd love to tell you about sometime."

Summer gave me a long, silent beat before an emotionless "I look forward to it."

"Great!" I was practically bouncing with the thought. "But I guess we should focus on the here and now, right? Like what kinda tools we need, food . . ."

"And sleep," added Summer.

"Say what?"

"The day's almost half over"—Summer gestured to the wall clock—"and you need a full night's sleep before heading to the Nether."

"Can't we just sleep there?" I asked.

"If you want your bed to explode." Before I could react, she held up a silencing hand. "That's what the manual I found said, and whether the author was having a laugh or not, I'm not exactly eager to find out."

"I'll take your . . . their word for it." *Exploding beds?!* What else was waiting in this strange new land?

"It's for the best anyway," continued Summer in what I now recognized as her signature "all-business" tone. "It'll give us time to brew."

"Brew?" I thought I knew what she meant. "Like the kind of stuff folks drank in our world that made them giggly and stumbly and sometimes vomity?"

"Not exactly," said Summer, leading me along the balcony. "No, these potions are more like the night-vision, fast-feet, fire-proof kind."

"Get out," I scoffed, not wanting to believe something so cool. "You are not talking about superpowers."

"Just wait and see," teased Summer as she went into a room made entirely of that black-speckled white stone (later, I learned from one of Summer's books that it's called "diorite"). At first, I thought it was another bathroom, because the first thing I noticed was a four-by-four pond of water in the corner. But as Summer moved aside, I saw a strange new device next to the pond. The center was a horizontal rod, one block high, with an orange color brightening to yellow. Around it were three stands, flat stone bases above empty metal clasps.

"This is a brewing stand," explained Summer, reaching into

one of the room's storage chests. "This is where I make these." She produced a small transparent bottle, the kind I'd accidentally made myself when first experimenting with glass. But the liquid inside . . . I'd only been able to fill my bottles with water, and what's the point if you don't get dehydrated? But this brew, this pinkish potion, it shimmered and glowed!

"I think this one will do," she said, and led me back the way we came, through her bedroom, down the stairs, across the main chamber floor, and all the way to the mountain's exit.

"What kind of potion is this?" I asked impatiently as she opened the double doors. As the blast of hot air engulfed us, I realized that Summer wasn't going back for the lava lever. She just stood there, barely a block from the molten curtain.

Lifting the bottle to her lips, she said, "Watch and"—gulp, gulp, gulp—"learn."

And then she stepped into the lava!

"Summer!" I rushed forward, reaching out, burning the tips of my fingers. "Summer, don't . . ."

"Don't worry." That laugh, clear and bright just beyond the flames. "I'm fine."

And she was! Stepping out of the firefall, gently nudging me back. She wasn't hurt, not even singed! And her hands on my chest felt cool to the touch!

"Whoa . . ." I gasped, and added a poetic, "That is so awesomely . . . awesome!"

"Potion of fire resistance," she declared, brandishing the empty bottle. "One of many we can brew."

"We can?" was all I could think to ask. "Can I try?" I must

have sounded like a little kid, and I don't blame Summer for laughing. But I mean, c'mon! Magic potions? Tell me you wouldn't be losing it too!

"Come on then," said Summer, leading me back to her laboratory (or "labor-atory," as she pronounced it).

Okay, now, if you already know how to brew potions, you can probably skip this part; I won't be offended, I guess. But if you don't, if you've never combined elements to create drinkable superpowers, listen very carefully to how it's done.

First, you need the basic raw materials: glass bottles, water, and something called "nether wart." It's a kind of red fungus-y thing that grows in . . . you guessed it, the Nether, although Summer'd transplanted some to a "dark farm" room in her mountain.

The brewing stand works pretty much like every other appliance in this world. There's a chamber up at the top for your ingredient and three chambers at the bottom for your bottles.

All I had to do was place the nether wart above, and the bottles and the brewing stand did the rest.

The result didn't look much different than water. Summer explained it was just a "mundane potion," the basic foundation for whatever power I wanted to add. That came with a variety of different ingredients.

To name just a few, something called "magma cream" gave you fire resistance, puffer fish let you breathe underwater, and sugar—just plain old sugar—gave your legs the speed of an arrow.

Okay, maybe I'm exaggerating just a tad. But it sure did feel that way! I placed the handful of white granules in the brewing stand's top slot, watched the bubbling reaction, and lifted the now bluish, shimmering bottle up for Summer's approval.

"Why stop at level one," she asked, running out of the room.

"There's another level?!" I called after her, and was answered with the distant creak of a storage chest.

"Just pop in a pinch of glowstone," she said, trotting back into the room with a handful of the precious substance. "I know it's a bit of a waste, but soon we'll have more than we need."

The glowstone went in. The brewing stand bubbled.

"Well, what are you waiting for?" she asked, turning for the door. I followed her back down the hallway to the front doors, and waited as she switched off the lava. "Don't go too far," Summer warned, as the burning curtain gave way to arctic chill. "The potion won't last too long. You haven't added any redstone for duration."

I should have asked if we could do that, head back up to the lab and mix in that extra, time-extending ingredient. But time was something I didn't want to think about at that moment.

Patience. Sometimes it's a voice I just don't want to hear.

Glug, glug, glug.

It tasted sweet—no doubt the sugar, with the slightest carbonated bite.

"I don't feel any different," I said, looking down at my feet. What did I expect? Wings on my shoes?

"It won't until you run." Summer began shooing me out the door. "So have a go!"

I took a cautious step forward, then another, and a third, and . . .

"WHOA!"

I was racing, jetting across the snow! I was a superhero, a god from ancient mythology! I didn't care about the freezing air up my nose, stinging my eyes and lungs. Magic! Speed!

"Yeeeaaaah!" I shouted, my voice rushing to catch up. "Woohoooo!"

I glanced to my left, then my right, breathless at the sight of the land racing by. Like through the window of a car or an express train. Trees and hills galloping past my field of vision.

Suddenly a dark mass rose up ahead of me. The forest! How far had I gone? How much ground had I covered in just a few ecstatic seconds!

Where was I? Back where I'd met Summer? Where was the igloo?

Another glance to either side, just a moment of not watching where I was going.

Bonk!

There it was, smashed into my flat face.

"Ugh," I groaned, backing up from the sudden obstacle. I wasn't damaged. I even laughed. Nothing was gonna spoil this mood.

"Awesome," I said aloud, then repeated in a shout, "AweSOME!" up to the—

Setting sun!

I took off for the mountain, thinking I'd be there in another few super-seconds.

But then . . .

Have you ever seen a cartoon where a rabbit eats special carrots to become a superhero? I know I have. And while I can't remember much about the plot, I do recall a moment in the story when, mid-flight, he literally runs out of power with the sputtering choke of an airplane.

PUTT-PUTT-FFFVVVVVV.

That sound ran through my mind as the potion wore off and the streaking world around me slowed to a creeping crawl.

"Not good," I said, as the sun dipped below the horizon. What had Summer said about going too far? What was my own lesson about friends listening?

No problem, I thought, shivering with the plummeting temperature. *I can just walk the rest of the way.*

GRRRP!

That was my stomach.

Running had burned up more than the potion.

Again, *no problem*, as I reached into my belt for a snack.

Nothing.

And I mean nothing.

Not just no food; no tools, no weapons, and, as another shiver reminded me, not even any armor. Everything was back in the guest room storage chest. I'd gone out into the open with nothing but painted-on clothes and thoughtless verve!

"Guuugh!"

That was not my stomach.

I spun in a 180. The zombie was right behind me!

"Guuugh!"

It lunged. I dodged.

"Guuugh!" Another one to my left.

I ran for the mountain, which now felt like walking in molasses. Hungry, cold, and . . .

THWACK!

Hurt! An arrow in my shoulder.

Don't panic, I told myself, zigzagging as more arrows stabbed the air around me. *I can make it. Just keep focused, keep aware.*

A creeper appeared suddenly, right in front of me, with a telltale hiss.

I jumped!

The blast hit me midair, throwing me forward. Pain!

Almost there . . .

"Guuugh!" More zombies, blinking into existence, barring my way to the mountain.

Keep moving! But right or left?

Panic threatened to overwhelm me as I saw another mob behind the zombies. Smaller. One of those halfling ghouls?!

No! Not smaller—farther away. But coming up fast!

Summer!

Whisking between my undead blockers, diamond sword flashing in the moonlight.

"Here!" she shouted, tossing me two potions.

The first was vile, way too salty with an acid burn. It felt like I'd licked a corroding battery, but a split second later, I couldn't have cared less. In a flash, really, all my wounds were gone!

Instant health!

"Whoa," I said, savoring the bottled miracle. "This stuff is really awe—"

"Oi!" Summer shouted, slashing one of the zombies to smoke. "Drink the other one!"

I didn't have to ask what that other one was. As soon as the bubbly sweetness ran down my throat, I lightning-bolted back to the mountain.

"Aw yeeaaah!" Past spiders and creepers and glacially slow zombies. "Come and get me!"

Skidding to a halt in front of the mountain's open front doors, I turned to shout another taunt at my sluggish pursuers. The words never came.

"What did I tell you?!" Summer's face in mine. She must have been a half-step behind me. "What were you thinking?!"

"I . . . wasn't?" I said, eyes down, joy deflating.

"Bloody right!" she spat, with a chorus of mob sounds behind her. "C'mon."

The doors clicked behind us. I stood there silently, watching her flick the lava lever. "Look, I'm . . . I'm sorry, all right? I've just never felt anything like that."

"I understand, I—"

"I'm sorry, Summer, I'm sorry, I really am!"

"It's all right!" she half-barked, half-chuckled. "Once is enough, for heaven's sake."

And as I absorbed fresson six—Friends only have to apologize once—Summer continued, "I felt the same way the first time I learned to brew. I understand that they can make you feel so invincible that you lose your mind for a bit."

I nodded vigorously.

"I just need you to understand that that can't happen down in the Nether."

"It won't," I promised.

"I trust you," she said with a lighthearted laugh, and handed me a stack of flattened cookies. "Let's get you fed and off to bed. We've got a big day tomorrow."

Cookies for dinner. Right up there with magic potions. I

scarfed them down as Summer walked me to my room. "I'll check your kit in the morning," she said, pausing at the door, "and make sure you have all the potions you need."

"Shouldn't you tell me a little bit more about what's down there?" I asked. "You know, so I can learn about what to expect."

"You'll learn when we're there," said Summer, but then she added, "I trust you not to lose your head down there, right?"

I nodded.

"Then trust me to tell you what you need to know when you need to know it."

"I trust you," I said, as the door closed between us.

Fresson seven: Friends trust each other.

CHAPTER 9

Those fressons were still on my mind as I woke up the next morning, loaded my gear, armed and armored myself, and nibbled a cookie on the way to meet Summer in the main chamber.

"Morning, partner," she said.

Partner! We were partners now!

"You all kitted out?" She looked me over. "Food, arrows, tools, extra spider silk to repair your bow?"

"Everything I'll need," I answered, "except . . ."

"Potions galore." Summer passed me a dozen shimmering bottles. "All enhanced and extended," she said, and handed over a few bottles of plain water. "You don't technically 'need' these, per se, but in that kind of heat, a good drink of water does wonders for your spirits."

"It's hot down there?" My spirits were already lifting. "That'll be a welcome change from the cold."

Summer laughed. "You might not think so after the first second or two." She led me to a pair of steel doors, the only steel doors in the entire mountain, and said, "I have to keep this one locked, just in case the odd baddie tries following me back."

"Baddie?" I asked, but got only the flicking lever for an answer.

As the iron door swung open, I followed Summer into a plain, gray stone room that held the strangest object I'd ever seen by far. A giant frame, four by four of nothing but obsidian blocks. But instead of a picture, this frame encased a curtain of energy. At least, that's the best way I can describe it. Swirling, purplish pink eddies attracted glowing violet flakes that seemed to appear out of nowhere. And the sound: a high, echoing rasp. Was it breathing? Was it alive?

"The portal?"

"The portal."

Even at this range, a half-dozen blocks away, I could feel the pulsing power. Vibrating my teeth, tingling the roots of my hair.

And my nose, wrinkling at the subtle stink.

"Netherrack?"

Summer nodded. "The portal is always open. Which is why you feel the heat as well."

Which I could. Radiating from the gate. Hot and dry like a desert breeze.

"It won't be pleasant," warned Summer, taking a step closer to the gate, "especially if you're prone to motion sickness."

Was I? I couldn't remember from my old life. Did I get sick

in cars? Planes? I hadn't felt anything on minecarts or boats—which I suspect don't count because the ocean is tabletop-smooth.

"You might feel the urge to move," continued Summer. "Don't. It will break the transfer. Stay absolutely still, and know that it'll all be over in just a few seconds."

"Got it," I said with way more certainty than I felt.

"Together then," declared Summer, "on my mark."

I stood next to her, ready for that first, last step.

"Three," she counted, "Two . . ."

Oh why won't this world let us hold hands when we're scared?!

"One!"

I stepped into the vortex. Vision swimming, skin prickling, stomach contents rising up through my vibrating chest.

I tried to breathe, but the air was hot and stifling, with that horrible stench blasting up my nose.

The rasp in my ears. Loud. Deafening. I fought the urge to move. Forced my body to freeze.

The wavy, sickening image of Summer's portal room blinked into solid purple. Then, suddenly another image, dark and rusty with vertical orange lines.

"Move now!" I heard Summer call, and took a couple wobbly steps forward.

"Stop!"

I halted.

"Look down."

I did. I was standing at the edge of a cliff, high above an ocean, an actual ocean . . . of lava! I backed up hurriedly, crashing into Summer.

"Mind the gate," she barked, but I was far too dazed to respond.

"I can't . . ." I started to say, but lost the thought in coughing.

"Just take a moment to orient yourself," said Summer, stepping in front of my face. "The heat, the smell—you'll get used to it, I promise."

"What about my eyes?" I asked, looking past her into the permanent twilight.

"They're fine," she answered calmly. "It's this world."

I realized, a second later, what she meant. Up close, I could see Summer perfectly. It was the land around us that threw me.

Netherrack. Spreading out into what looked like a giant cavern.

And the heat! She wasn't kidding. An oven under my armor, against my skin, in my lungs. An arid fierceness that pulled the moisture from my body, drying my eyes, my throat. I tried to swallow. Another cough.

"Here." Summer offered me a bottle of water. "Told you it would help."

She was right. I'd never been thirsty before, never craved liquid like I did at that moment. "Pity our bodies can't just sip," mused Summer as I gulped down every welcome drop. "Since quenching our thirst doesn't do anything more than lift our spirits. Wouldn't it be nice to ration that kind of mental tonic?" Packing away the empty bottle, I saw that she now held a bow, and that her eyes were darting past me in all directions.

"What are you looking for?" I asked, reaching for my own arrow launcher.

"I'll tell you if it shows up," she said, swapping her bow for a potion. "But right now, let's have a proper look-see."

That was the potion she was drinking now.

Night vision.

I reached in my belt for an identical, pink-shimmering bottle. It didn't taste too bad—like fizzy, metallic carrot juice.

I gulped it down quickly, then caught my breath as the entire world lit up around me.

The rusty haze melted away into a misty pink. It was a cavern. An underground world! I could see that the sparse, glowing, vertical lines were actually streams of lava, pouring from the netherrack ceiling into the molten ocean below.

Netherrack mountains—more like giant stalagmites—rose from the burning sea to connect with the roof above. And connecting them all was a central, broken plain. That's where we stood now, at the mid-level on a small scrap of land no bigger than half a dozen cubes.

"Can't blame me for our landing site," said Summer. "The world just happened to place the portal atop this floating island. You don't get to choose where you end up."

Island? Floating island?

I looked up to spot other patches of suspended netherrack, just hanging in midair, like the first time I punched out the bottom of a tree. And we were standing on one! A dust speck above an ocean of fire.

"Whoa, boy," I groaned dizzily. As if the heat and smell weren't bad enough, this new night vision made me feel like a tightrope walker who didn't realize he was on a tightrope till someone turned on the lights.

"Not to worry," Summer said, pointing to something behind me, "we're still firmly connected to the mainland."

By "firmly connected," she meant a very long, very thin, very terrifying strip of double netherrack that ran from our speck to the edge of the main plain.

You gotta be kidding me, I thought, stomach rebelling worse than after a lunch of zombie flesh.

"Let's be off," chirped my partner, striding confidently toward what immediately struck me as "Death-trap Bridge."

"Uh, Summer," I said, looking past her at the precarious walkway. "I have this thing . . . a phobia, you see . . . well . . . I guess it's not technically a phobia if phobias are things you fear that can't really hurt you, you know, like those little spiders back home with creepy long legs but jaws that are actually too small to—"

"Guy!" Summer cut me off. "What are you going on about?"

I stammered, realizing that I was facing two challenges at once. Not just crossing the bridge, but admitting I might be too afraid to do it!

I'd never been in this situation before. There'd been no one around to see my weakness. What would she think of me if I totally wimped out?

"There was"—I fought through a shaking, drying throat— "there was this lava, a lake of it . . . under my island, and . . ."— stinging nose, evaporating tears—"and . . ."

"You fell in," said Summer, stepping right up next to me. "Join the club. I've had more than my share of burn baths." She laughed, that wonderful, comforting laugh. "The first time was on the surface, right into a lava pond while I was gathering it for my first hot tub." I could feel her breath on my face, cooler than the air. "And you best believe, the memories of that first sizzle are always on my mind down here."

"So . . . you're afraid too?"

Another symphonic laugh. "Of course! Who wouldn't be down here? And if we don't admit our fears to each other, how can we help each other?"

More tears, but this time, they were tears of relief.

Fresson eight: Friends shouldn't be afraid to admit their fears.

Summer pivoted to stand next to me, pressing her armored shoulder against mine. "You'll be all right," she said in a reassuring tone. "If I thought otherwise, I'd give you one of our fireproof potions."

"Maybe," I said, reaching into my belt, "just in case . . ."

"You can do this." Her voice solid, confident. "Just keep breathing, keep your eyes on me, and I'll get us across safely."

"Promise?" I squeaked.

"Promise." She handed me another bottle of water.

It helped. Both the water and her conviction. *How did I ever make it so long by myself?* "I'm ready," I declared with all the real and fake courage I could muster. "Let's do this."

"Onward then." Summer turned for the bridge as I tried not to look down.

Lava everywhere!

I could feel the heat blasting up around us. It was like walking over a giant hair dryer.

How many steps?

A couple dozen? An eternity.

So high!

Even if it hadn't been lava, the fall alone would have been enough to . . . to what? What does death look like for block people like us? Would I have been smashed into pulp or just poofed into smoke like everything else? And would there be anything left behind? Some of my gear, or just an empty space, as if I'd never been?

"Courage is a full-time job," I whispered, reciting one of my hardest-learned lessons over and over again to bolster myself. "Courage is a full-time job."

"What's that?" Summer asked over her shoulder.

"Nothing!" I gulped as the lava popped below me. "Just one of my lessons."

"Hm," she responded over her shoulder, "like the one I think comes from my home."

"What's that?"

"Who dares, wins."

"Hey," I said, about to compliment her on such a witty phrase, then yelled another "Hey!" as I realized that we'd crossed over onto wide, safe ground.

"See"—Summer turned to face me—"I knew you could do it. I believe in you."

She believed in me!

"We won't be going far today," she said, heading for what looked like a solid wall. "What we're after is just on the other side."

"Is this a whole new planet," I asked, "or another land under the first one?"

"Probably the latter," she answered, "but I wouldn't try digging up to the surface from here."

"How come?"

My question got a pausing turn. "My second burn bath," she said, pointing to a lava fall that rolled down a distant hill. "Shower, actually. My first time digging for glowstone I picked one block above me too many."

"Yikes!" I shivered in the heat. "Do you think there's another ocean of lava above us?"

"I'm in no great hurry to find out," answered Summer, continuing a few more steps before she announced, "Here we are then." We were standing at the edge of the wall, next to a single doorway I hadn't seen.

"Stay behind me," she said, reaching for her bow. "And be ready to run if I tell you."

Run from what?

I followed her down the narrow, suffocating tunnel and to an exit that caused a pause with raised arrow. Was something waiting for us out there?

"Stay here," she commanded, then stepped out into the open. I thought I heard something—faint footsteps and a strangled, quick snort. It didn't seem to bother Summer, though. She looked right, then left, then let out an audible sigh. "Right then," she chirped, stowing her weapons, "all clear."

I sighed in response, exited the tunnel, turned left to follow her, and nearly crashed right into the most hideous creature I'd ever seen!

A zombie! A pig zombie! No, seriously! This thing, this . . .

abominable abomination, for lack of a better term, looked like somebody had mixed ghoul and swine with a healthy dose of nightmare for good measure. Rotten, pink flesh. Gray bones under open, green-bordered wounds.

And the smell! Rotting bacon.

"Uuugh," it groaned, turning its crossed, dead eyes toward me.

A gold sword flashed in the dull pink haze.

I jumped back, reaching for my own blade.

"Wait!" shouted Summer, jumping in between me and the creature. "Don't do it!"

"Are you crazy?!" I yelled. "You're gonna get—"

"It won't attack!" Summer nudged me gently away. "And if you did, you'd bring the lot of them down on us!"

"I don't under—" I started to say, but shut up when Summer moved out of my way. There were more of them, five roaming "pork of the living deads," all wearing pieces of golden armor, all carrying golden swords.

"The first time I came down here," explained Summer, "I did exactly what you were about to do. I killed one, attracted its mates, and led them all right back through the portal into my mountain." She shook her head at the strange creatures before us. "I learned too late that they're harmless if left alone." She turned to face me. "But now you understand why I've got iron doors blocking the portal room. Just in case one of them decides to take a stroll. Even an accident can provoke them. A stray arrow, or a blow meant for something else . . ."

"Something else?" I asked, feeling my nausea return. "What else is—" My question abruptly halted in the face of a new one.

I pointed my fist at the zombie pigman's feet. "Is it the heat or the potion making me see something?"

"Neither," answered Summer. "Its gold boots are, in fact, glowing."

"Glowing with what?"

"Can't say. Some sort of magic, I guess." She motioned to the other zombie pigmen. Some of their armor and swords also had a luminous sheen.

"Magic?" I asked.

"Must be." My partner was surprisingly nonchalant about the whole thing.

"Aren't you curious about what kind?"

"Somewhat"—Summer shrugged—"but unless you know how to politely ask for a quick borrow, I don't see as we have any other safe options."

"I guess not," I conceded as the glowing-booted beast blundered away.

Magic! First potions and now items!

"Have you ever found others?" I asked Summer. "Tools and weapons, I mean? Other enchanted stuff up on the surface?"

"Not yet," said Summer flatly, "and, sadly, no way yet to make them."

All the more reason to keep going, I thought, watching the glowing boots recede into the mist. *There have to be more magic items up there, and ways to make them if they weren't just freely floating about. It just wouldn't be fair if they only exist in this h . . .*

I couldn't finish the word, even in my own head. It was a

rude word, especially among those of my people who believed a place like this existed as punishment after death.

At least I'm pretty sure that's what some folks believed. I don't know if I ever did myself, but I could see why others did. I mean, if someone spent their life choosing to hurt others, wouldn't it be kinda just if they spent their afterlife in a dark, hot, monster-filled pain-cave like this? In fact, I think, back home, there was even an expression where an experience is so bad they describe it as being welcomed to a place just like this.

If I'd discovered the Nether on my own, I probably would have avoided it like surface mobs avoid the sun.

But I wasn't on my own and I'd made a promise to help Summer. Fresson four: Friends keep their promises. In fact, don't people say in my world that the very expression of friendship is following someone into a place exactly like this?

So, while my guts were shouting "Check, please!" all I could do was catch my breath, straighten my back, and ask Summer, "So where do we go from here?"

CHAPTER 10

"This way," said Summer, striding across the netherrack desert. We skirted the occasional pit and random fire, and every half-minute or so, Summer would just stop, put up her hand for silence, and listen to the still, stinking air.

The one time I asked what she was trying to hear, all I got back was, "Hopefully, nothing." Eventually, we came to one of those giant, sloping columns that rose up and into the distant roof. As we turned the corner, I blinked hard at something that couldn't exist.

Snow blocks? Two lines of them, spaced roughly a dozen or so blocks apart, and intersecting in the middle of another open plain.

"Is that—"

"No," answered my clairvoyant partner. "It's actually a local mineral called nether quartz, and its contrast makes for an excellent landmark." I noticed that each smooth pale block was topped with a torch and that the intersection was also marked with four wooden signposts.

"It's really easy to get lost here," Summer continued. "Just check your compass."

I did. The needle spun and jerked like it was trying to find its way home.

"Same goes for maps. Blank ones suddenly look like someone's thrown drippy brown and gray paint down their faces. And those 'you' arrows in the middle twirl as madly as compass needles."

"So," I said, shaking my head, "in addition to falling into lava and maybe having a whole horde of zombie ghouls after you . . ."

"Getting lost is a serious threat," Summer completed the thought. "Believe me."

I believed her, and respected her even more. First the taiga, now the Nether. Ice, then fire. *Is there a challenge Summer can't conquer?* I marveled as we approached the collection of signposts.

The left one read "Mined out," the right "Low-hanging fruit." And then there was the "Ice Cube" sign directly in front of us, which seemed like a joke.

"What's that?" I asked, pointing to that third sign.

"You'll see eventually," said Summer, turning for "Mined out."

"The sign's not technically true," she said, heading down the trail of nether quartz. "There's this one pesky deposit I could never manage to reach safely."

She pointed up, far up, to a bright spot in the roof above. There it was. Glowstone! A cluster of yellow, luminous blocks.

"They used to be all over this bit," explained Summer. "When I first arrived, they dotted the roof like clouds."

"It's beautiful," I said, wondering what this place must have looked like then.

"It was easy enough to grab most of them," continued Summer, "but this one stubborn little bit just kept taunting me for ages."

"Do you really need it?" I asked, not challenging but genuinely curious. "I mean, couldn't we finish our mission faster if we just moved on to easier pickings?"

"Well . . ." Another unusual, very un-Summerly pause. Then, "If all you care about is the easy way of doing things . . ."

"What? No!" Suddenly I felt very defensive. "No way. I'm totally up for anything."

"Then you can help me finish my 'ramp.'" Summer nodded, lowering her fist to what I originally had thought was a hill. Looking closer, I saw it was more of a ramp, a staircase to nowhere that ended abruptly halfway to the roof.

"I never managed to get this finished," she said, "not before one of them showed up."

"'Them'? Who's 'them'? Is that what you keep looking for? One of 'them'?"

"Brehhh."

That wasn't Summer. The sound came from far away.

"What . . ." I started to ask.

"Shhh!" Summer raised her bow, twisting in all directions like my crazy compass needle.

"Brehhh." There it was again, a high, crackling wheeze, like air leaking out of a bag.

"Get your bow," whispered Summer, "and watch for anything moving."

My bow was already out, and my eyes already scanning the haze.

Another sound, a strange, eerie twitter. "Wehwehwoowoo."

I whispered just one word: "What?" And got just one word in reply.

"Ghast."

"Wehwehwoowoo."

"You never know when you'll spot one," whispered Summer. "And you have to spot them first!"

The tension in her voice was the first I'd heard since we met. Summer, the tough, no-nonsense warrior, who seemed to have everything figured out, was worried now, which made me positively freaked.

"OooOoo" went a high wail, rising, then falling in the cotton-candy mist.

"Look everywhere," whispered Summer. "Up, down—they can come from anywhere."

"What do they look like?" I gulped, cowering behind my shaking bow.

"They float," she answered, turning slowly in a full circle, "like giant balloons."

The ethereal twittering began again, sending my teeth chattering.

"It's under us"—Summer's eyes fell—"the space between land and lava." Her bow dipped slightly, coming to rest at the line where the plains ended at a cliff. "Watch for it rising."

I tried, matching my aim to hers.

A few seconds, waiting. Holding my breath for what seemed like hours.

"OooOoo." Fainter this time, farther away.

"It's leaving." Summer sighed, lowering her weapon. "We've got a bit of time."

She took off running for the staircase. I followed with a mouthful of questions.

Where had it gone? What did it take to kill one? What could they do to us?

I didn't get a chance to ask. Summer was already tossing me a stack of netherrack. "Quickly! It'll be back soon!"

I watched her rush over to the edge of the unfinished staircase, just beneath the wall that ended in the highest step. "Do as I do," she commanded, then jumped straight up and placed a netherrack block beneath her.

Genius, I thought, repeating the same action next to her. So simple. Jump and place. Why hadn't I ever thought of that? We hopped atop our rising columns just past the last step.

"Brill!" commented Summer, looking at the nearly reachable glowstone. "Only three to go!"

We rushed down the staircase, around to the edge, and repeated the process. "I'm almost out of netherrack," I said, looking at my dwindling stock.

"Just take some from the bottom," she said, racing to stack a third column.

Duh!

Grabbing my pickaxe, I started chopping at the center base.

The crunchy, purplish material gave little resistance. Less than stone or even dirt. Within seconds, netherrack cubes were flying into my belt.

"Hurry up then!" called Summer from the top of her newly finished step. "We're almost finished!"

"Be right there," I hollered, and hop-placed the new blocks up to meet her.

"There we go!" she chirped, standing next to the glowing cubes. "You harvest, I'll keep watch."

As Summer, bow in hand, turned to scour our surroundings, I turned my pickaxe on the dozen or so blocks of glowstone. The first one shattered with the sound of breaking glass as three yellow pinches jumped into my pack.

"Don't worry if some fall," said Summer to my back. "We'll get them on the way down."

"Got it," I said as another tri-stack of powder fell beyond my grasp.

"And you might want to place some netherrack around the bottom of the deposit," she continued. "That way you can mine from different ang—"

That eerie chittering again, drawing closer.

"Don't stop!" snapped Summer, who must have instinctively known I was going to turn.

"It'll be here any second!"

"Wehwehwoowoo!"

Closer now. Louder.

Summer's "Faster!" scared me back to furious picking.

Another block shattered into powder, then another. How many more to go?

"Brrrehh!" A birdlike chirp, the rolling Rs seeming almost gleeful in anticipation, rose to a piercing screech!

I couldn't help but turn. Just in time to see Summer, bow swapped for sword, swinging at something approaching.

A fireball! An actual burning missile, which she batted away like she was hitting a home run!

"Just hit a six," she huffed cryptically, and then, switching back to a bow, caught me looking at her and roared, "PICK!"

I did, spinning to assault the few remaining blocks.

Wheezing wails rang in my ears, punctuated by the whip of Summer's arrow. She must have missed, because I thought I heard her grunt something angry like "Muddy bell!"

Another wheezing "Brchhh," rising to a shrieking "Breee-aaaa!" And the sound-popping flames grew in my ears.

It must have been that distraction, coupled with my al-ready frayed nerves, that caused my next, nearly fatal mistake. Hearing the THONK of Summer sword-batting, I picked out the last of the glowstone blocks, then kept going for just the barest of moments, before my brain commanded my hand to stop.

Too far! The crunchy, delicate netherrack behind it fell away, revealing an orange, incandescent wall.

"Lava!"

I could have just blocked it up, and would have if my brain had been working.

Panic drowns thought.

"RUN!"

I spun, bashing into Summer, shoving her frantically down the stairs.

"What the blo . . ." she started to say, then looked past me and took flight.

That uncanny cry sounded again, just to my right.

The ghast! A giant, pale head atop stubby, dangling tentacles. Black slitted eyes opening to round red holes.

"Breeeaaaa!"

The red, open mouth, a missile launcher ready to rain down fire.

"Jump!" Summer leapt off the staircase. I should have. But mind reeling, feet fixed, I just stood there stupidly and raised my quivering shield.

Boom!

Blown off the staircase. Coughing and flying through the air. Landing on cracked ankles beside Summer.

I took a moment to breathe, get my bearings, figure out my next move.

"What are you doing?!" Another blow, this time from her, punching me on the back, driving me into action. "The lava!"

I'd totally forgotten. Another second and I would have been doused in death.

"Across the pit!" Summer cried, jumping in and out of a slight depression ahead of us.

"Breeeaaaa!" The blast hit me square in the back, burning through armor, hammering bones, throwing me into the depression of now burning netherrack.

Fire.

Choking, gasping, blinking through flames.

"Guy!" called Summer as an arrow whistled over my head. "This way!"

Running to catch up, meeting her behind the pillar's bend.

"Drink!" A shimmering bottle in my face. The salty sting of insta-health.

"Better?"

"Better," I breathed, still amazed by how quickly these potions worked. "Thank you!"

"Here," she said, handing me another night-vision potion. "The first dram's almost out, and we'll need to top off again before we attack."

"Attack?" Suddenly, I didn't feel so good anymore. "You want to kill the ghast?"

"No." She turned to look me in the eye. "You will."

"WhahowIwhoa," I stammered, as another creepy call echoed from around the corner.

"You can do it, Guy." Summer's voice was confident, although I thought I detected a hint of annoyance, too. "Just sneak up behind it for a kill shot while I draw its fire."

"But why?" I yipped. "Why mess with it at all? We got what we came for! Let's just get outta here!" I didn't feel ashamed this time. I didn't see any point in fighting.

"Guy"—Summer took a deep, calming breath—"you need to know how to handle a ghast, and everything else down here, if you're going to be of any help." Another deep breath. "I can't always be taking care of you. We have to be able to take care of each other, understand?"

Why did she have to be right? Why did I need a new fresson right now?

This wouldn't be our last ghast. And if I didn't learn how to deal with them now, I'd be nothing but a constant burden. She was right.

Fresson nine: Friends take care of each other.

"Fine," I huffed as another ghastly screech filled my ears. "Just tell me what I gotta do."

"What I already told you," Summer counter-huffed. "Just wait for me to get out there and take the heat. When you see its back turned, draw your bow and pop the little blighter like a balloon!"

"But what if it turns toward m—"

Summer was already gone, sword in hand, rushing into the open with a fearless shout of "Here I am!"

"Breeeaaaa!" I poked my head around just in time to see the creature launch another fireball.

Summer didn't try to bat it back. Instead she just dodged, darting away as the bombshell detonated harmlessly at her side. "Poor little gasbag!" She laughed, then broke into a song about, of all things, a running rabbit.

"Breeeaaaa!"

More fireballs. More near-misses. Summer zigzagging in a semicircle to turn the ghast's face away from me.

"Run, rabbit! Run, rabbit! Runrunrun!"

Her courage, her calm. I probably wasted half a minute just staring in awe before getting my head together.

I stepped out into the open, drew my bow, and tried to line up my shot. Despite the creature's size and apparent slowness, it was a pretty slippery target. The way it rose and fell, drifted this way and that, made it difficult to track.

WHHP!

My first shot fell just beneath its tentacles.

"Aim higher!" shouted Summer, dodging another impact. "Shoot where it's going to be!"

I loaded her advice into the second arrow, trying to anticipate my target's course.

WHHP!

Another miss, to the right just as it floated left.

"You'll get it! Keep shooting!" Summer's voice, her conviction. She believed in me.

I drew my bow again, held my breath, then gasped as the hideous chalky blimp turned slowly in my direction. Black slitted eyes became red and the closed line mouth rounded for a launch.

"SHOOT!"

WHHP!

"Breeaaaa!"

We fired our shots, and dodged, at the same time. It missed. I didn't.

A faint pop. A crackling hiss. The ghast disappeared as something small, light, and faintly oval fell to the ground at Summer's feet.

"Ghast tear," she said, running forward to show me the crystalline prize, "the prime ingredient for a regeneration potion. A little different from insta-health, but I'll explain that later."

"Cool," I said, still trying to process what had just happened.

"You take it," she said, handing me the trophy. "You deserve it." Then, punching me lightly on the shoulder, she announced, "Guy! You killed your first ghast!"

"Yeah," I answered, nodding my head with the realization, "I did, didn't I?"

A hug might have been in order, but a fist bump would do for now.

"I knew you could!" Her words made me feel ten blocks tall.

"So where do we go now?" I asked, ready for anything this new broiling realm could throw at me.

"Back to the mountain," said Summer, turning for the quartz path. "I think we've had quite enough victories for one day."

"Really?" I couldn't believe how disappointed I felt. "We can't keep going?"

"We need to rest," warned Summer, "and celebrate! We just proved we can take care of each other! Which means we're stronger together. We're a team now, Guy."

"I guess we are," I nodded, feeling like I'd drunk a potion of levitation.

Summer had touched on another fresson: Friends are stronger together. And that one set off a whole mental chain reaction. Why do we need friends? Not just for company, but for actual needs as well! Right? I'm sure, when we were huddling in the prehistoric trees, we weren't just saying, "Hey, dude, you're really cool. We should totally hang out." It was probably more like, "Dude, if we're gonna eat tonight, you watch for lions while I pick us some berries."

Maybe the actual language was different, probably a lot more like "oo-oo-ah-ah," but you get where I'm going. Friendship is a survival skill, in that time or ours. We might not have to watch for killer lions anymore, but we still have challenges. Big ones. Sometimes even dangerous ones. And it's a lot easier to face those challenges with someone else.

Fresson ten: Friends are stronger together.

CHAPTER 11

I didn't mind the purple swirl, or the dizzy, acid nose burps I got from traveling through the portal. I was on top of the world, literally, when we materialized back in Summer's mountain. Stepping out into the portal room, I blinked at the bright, dazzling colors of the main chamber. The blue pond, the green crops. And the air, cool and fresh in comparison to the thermal blast of down below. I would have just stood there for a few moments, venting my lungs, waiting for my body temperature to lower, but . . .

"Hurry!" Summer darted away from me, disappearing toward the front door.

"Wh . . ." I started to ask.

"Hurry!" her voice echoed down the hall. "While you're still too hot!"

Wondering what she had up her painted sleeve, I got to the exit just as she switched off the lava fall.

"Take off your armor!" she said, throwing open the doors. "You're going to love this!"

I'd just taken off my helmet and chest plate when the freezing air hit us.

"Oh yeah," I said, savoring the refreshing chill. "I see what you . . ."

But she was off again! Running across the snow, down to the frozen river!

"Oh no," I breathed. "You can NOT be—"

"Come on!" I watched her bound down the bank, out of sight, and heard a few quick PLINKS of pickaxe on ice.

"What are you waiting . . ." Summer began, and then, after an audible splash, finished with a breathy "f-f-for!"

"Crazy girl," I huffed, running after her. "And I gotta be crazier for following her!"

A few snow-crunching strides brought me down to the sight of Summer waist-deep in a hacked-out pond.

"Just do it!" she shouted. "Don't think!"

Don't think. As easy as not breathing!

But I tried not to do either, racing onto the ice and leaping into the air.

SMACK!

Down to the bottom, pushing up from the mud, I came up with an explosive "Bwaaaaa!"

"Isn't it glorious!" Summer asked as I splashed and gasped and tried to put subzero syllables into words.

"Yeeeaaayayaya . . ." was my grand answer.

"The first time I returned from the Nether"—Summer splashed me—"I was so hot I thought I'd snuff it. But then I remembered that some people back in our world—maybe in a country close to mine?—they pop from saunas to cold-water plunges for their health."

"Yehehyea," I shivered, "r-r-really h-h-healthy."

Summer laughed. So did I. Sharing a laugh with a friend—well, I considered *her* a friend, at least—was glorious.

"Nothing quite like returning from the Nether," continued Summer, "to really make you appreciate the world we live in up here."

I'm sure I would have answered with something equally insightful. I might even have quoted that lesson about being grateful for what we have, especially if what we have is something as wonderful as the natural world. The smell of a tree, the breeze on my face, the sight of high, white clouds floating lazily. Bright sun, blue sky. Amazing what you don't appreciate until it's gone. I'm sure I would have said something—

But my stomach beat me to the punch.

GRRRP.

"Guess you're hungrier than you realized," Summer teased, climbing out of the river. "The heat down there can make you forget to eat. And throw in all that running and fighting and I'm right on the edge of starvation."

She wasn't exaggerating. The river wasn't the only thing chilling me, and a whiff of my own unusually bad breath left no room for debate.

"I think a celebratory dinner is in order," announced Summer as we headed back for the mountain.

"Totally!" I chimed in.

Bread, baked potatoes, cookies . . .

"Chicken!" Summer practically flew through the doors as she spoke. "Nothing hits the spot like a bit of blackened bird!"

And suddenly I wasn't hungry anymore. Just the opposite. I felt sick, slammed with a looming confrontation I'd managed to avoid with the previous mutton breakfast.

"Well, come on then." Summer led me down the hall, across the main chamber, and through another set of double doors. "Let's feed them before they feed us!"

I swallowed spit, took another gulp of head-clearing air.

"The coop's just down this way." Summer was already in another door-lined hallway.

"Ummm . . ." I tried to speak, tried to think. How to get out of this. How to explain.

"What was that?" asked Summer, slowing her pace.

"Oh," I stammered, "I just—" At that moment, my eyes fell on an open door to my right, a dark, bare chamber with recessed redstone torches above a smooth stone floor, lined with . . . MUSHROOMS!

". . . just thought mushroom soup would be better!" I said with sudden confidence. "I mean, why go through all the trouble of killing and cooking when we can just pick—"

"Surely you jest," Summer laughed in my face. "Gooey mushroom slop? Never touch the stuff anymore, unless it goes in a rabbit stew." She made a little, musing "hm" at the thought. "Would you prefer that? A spot of hunting, a few hoppers in the pot with some carrots and—"

"No," I gulped. "No thanks."

"On then," she said, continuing her trot, "to the cluckers."

Outwardly, I was silent, but my brain was screaming in alarm.

She's going to be angry! When I tell her, she's going to be insulted and hurt! Maybe even throw me out!

"Here we are," she said, and opened a single door at the end of the hallway.

Just when we were starting to become friends! Had our first adventure together. Shared our first victory! Now this!

I followed her into a short, narrow chamber, nothing but some torches, another door in front, and a double chest cut into a side recess. "I usually feed them once a week," she said, opening the chest to remove two clumps of bright green wheat seeds. "Unless I'm really hungry."

If I just don't tell her . . . I thought, turning on my own guilt. *Just go along with it, just one more time.*

"There you go." Summer handed me a clump of stacked seeds, then backed up a few blocks from the next door. "Careful," she said, and drew an iron axe from her belt. "Sometimes they run out."

Don't risk upsetting her. Don't ruin everything!

The door slid open to a cacophony of clucks and an overwhelming smell of feathers.

When I'd raised chickens, it'd been outdoors. I never knew that enough of them in a small room carried a concentrated scent. It wasn't bad. Kind of like a pillow. I guess under normal circumstances, I might not have minded it, but in the state I was in now, with my spinning head and churning stomach . . . well, I don't want to imagine what I would've felt like if this world allowed them to poop.

There were about a dozen of them, pecking on the room's dirt floor or splashing in a central pond that even held a small island with a tree. "They do love their swim," said Summer, walking over to a wall lever, "and some fresh air."

Cн-cк!

Cold air rushed in from a pair of iron-grated holes in the wall. The crisp sensation seemed to perk me up, give me strength.

I can do this. Just go along with it. Swallow my feelings for a while.

Holding out the seeds, letting the birds peck their food from my hand.

It's better than losing Summer, right? Better to keep the peace and keep the friend.

Their eyes. Trusting little dots. Just like on my island. Just like the moment before I . . .

"That should do it," announced Summer as a quartet of little squawking chicks appeared. "Enough to replace the ones we harvest."

Just look away, pretend it's not happening.

The axe in her hand.

Why can't I be allowed to cover my ears?

The blade, passing to *me*?!

"You do the honors." Her voice, matter-of-fact, like she was plucking wheat.

Just a few swipes, quick. Then it'll all be over.

Stepping over to the first bird.

You can . . .

Looking up at me.

You . . .

The eyes . . .

"I can't!"

Spinning to Summer, dropping the axe.

"Pardon?"

Dry throat, beating heart, sweat dripping into my eyes.

"I can't! I'm sorry! I can't kill them! I can't kill anything for food! I used to. On my island. I raised chickens too. All tame and friendly and expecting me to take care of them and . . . I killed them, almost all of them. I let a few go, but I killed so many . . . and I couldn't live with it. I felt so guilty! And yeah, I know, it's kinda hypocritical 'cause I still need their feathers for arrows and I know I'll have to make a choice when those run out, and yeah, I ate the rabbit but it died by accident and the sheep was killed by a wolf, and yeah, if I was starving and if it was me or them, like when I had to catch those fish down in the mine, but as long as I'm not starving and I don't have to, then I just can't kill another living thing for food. I can't! I won't!"

Silence.

Then . . .

"Okay."

"Okay?"

Summer shrugged.

"If you don't want to eat meat, then don't eat meat."

"Oh."

"As long as you don't mind if I do."

"No"—I shook my head vigorously—"no, that's fine . . . as long as I don't have to watch you kill them."

"Of course not." Summer gestured to the door. "Wait outside, or even in the kitchen so you don't hear anything."

"Oh." Another beat of silence, my heart still clanging in my chest. "You're sure that's okay?"

"Why wouldn't it be?" asked Summer, calmly retrieving her axe. "As long as you respect my life choices, why wouldn't I respect yours?"

So simple. So obvious! Friends respect each other's life choices.

I turned for the door.

"And, Guy . . ."

Turning back.

"Next time, if you need to tell me something, why not just tell me instead of telling yourself a story in your head."

"Noted," I said, and shut the door.

Walking down the hall, I digested yet another fresson: Friends communicate. I'd imagined an entire conflict, trying to control the future instead of just risking it by being honest. And as I chewed more on that wisdom, I realized it was really just a side dish to the main course: Friends shouldn't be afraid to be honest with their friends. What kind of friendship is built on lies and secrets? How can someone really be your friend if they don't know who you are?

The notion was a feast for my brain. So much so that I recounted it all to Summer over dinner.

"And that's why friends shouldn't be afraid to be honest with their friends."

"You and your lessons," Summer laughed after her last bite of chicken.

"I never get tired of learning." I shrugged, reaching for another cookie. "And there's so much to learn now. Life in this mountain, life in the Nether, life with you."

"You'll get the hang of it." Summer made a subtle, pleasant noise that, in a world of facial expressions, probably would have translated to a smile. "You'll be an expert in no time."

CHAPTER 12

Remember, back on the island, when I talked about my first week of routine? Well, if you don't, it was the first time my random adventures had finally settled down into a predictable pattern.

That's what happened here. Only instead of a week, it was a whole month. You know how when you're watching a movie, and they compress time into quick shots that last a few seconds? What do they call that? A montage? Picture that. Me getting up every morning, meeting Summer for breakfast, then loading up on arrows and potions before heading down into the Nether for more glowstone.

We always headed in one direction: down the quartz-marked path to the intersection, then a sharp turn to the land of "Low-hanging fruit." Glowstone was everywhere, bunched in luminescent clusters. Sometimes we'd build a ramp. Sometimes we'd just climb a natural slope. Sometimes one of us would build a "jump tower," jumping in place and stacking netherrack beneath us, while the other one kept watch for ghasts.

And there were plenty of ghasts!

I think, looking back, I must have bagged at least ten of them in all. Mostly without any trouble. Sometimes completely on my own. I got pretty good at getting the drop on them, listening for the approaching chirp, sweeping the pink mist with a drawn bow. And when it came to hitting the target, I began to master the fine art of long-range ballistics. It's not easy, at first, to predict where the floating, bobbing bombers are heading. But after enough practice I really did get the hang of it.

I also got the hang of what it was like to live with someone else. Summer might have still refused to admit that we were "friends," but our "partnership" sure did fit the bill. We adventured together, ate together, swam in that ridiculous arctic river together. I didn't complain too much. I didn't want to upset her, like when I occasionally brought up what we'd do or where we'd go after leaving the mountain. Those times always earned me a terse "Can we just focus on the here and now?" I figured she was just being practical, so I kept our downtime conversation to stories about my life on the island. I know I talk too much, as you've probably figured out by now, but I tried to keep my stories short and funny. I loved to hear her laugh. I never could have guessed how important something like that was for survival. Comfort. Strength. I hadn't been this happy since that first quiet week on the island.

And the happier I got, the less I thought about moving on. I can admit that to myself, and to you, now. I wasn't really aware of it at the time. I hadn't intended it to be that way. In the beginning, everything we did, every new skill I perfected, got filed into that book in my brain labeled "Helpful Hints for the Journey Ahead." That book was always in my thoughts, along with dreams of what was waiting out there. The other taiga beyond the forest, and the jungle beyond that. And then the great unknown. New lands, new possibilities. And hopefully, as always, the chance of a way back home.

But as time went on, and each reassuringly routine day rolled into the next, that book got smaller and smaller. It might have disappeared altogether if what happened at the end of that otherwise monotonous month hadn't occurred.

We'd just come back from a particularly lucrative haul. We'd gathered enough glowstone to finish lamps for the workshop. We'd worked all day and through the night (according to Summer, whose internal clock was way better than mine), and so when we got back the next morning, both of us were craving sleep.

"Too bad the world won't let us turn in before nightfall," said Summer, dumping her glowstone in a workshop chest. "But I know the perfect way to perk up!"

"Aw c'mon," I moaned, as she took off running for the front door. "C'mon!"

I knew where she was going, and I was definitely not in the mood.

I'd gotten reasonably used to the heat down in the Nether, the constant thirst, feeling like I was slow-cooking under my armor. I'd even gotten used to both bad smells: rotting, bacon-y zombie pigs and, well, the other, constant stink of you know what. So, I really didn't see the use of an ice-cold river plunge, and Summer knew my feelings well.

"Oh don't be such a baby!" she taunted, as the CLICK of the lava switch filled the entrance hall. "You know you love it!"

She knew I didn't. Leaping through the freezing air into even more freezing water. If I hadn't been so tired, I would have just watched from the bank. But I went along with her, and the chill did invigorate me.

I was about to get back out for a hot shower when I felt something wriggle past my leg.

I yipped, splashing out of the way. I expected to see a squid; they were rare but not unknown in this river. Instead I caught sight of what could only be a . . .

"Fish!"

"Pardon?" Summer had ceased her splashing just long enough to hear me. "What are you on about?"

"Look!" I pointed to the small, swimming life-form. "Look, a fish!"

"Several," she corrected. There were at least three more, all swimming ahead of the one that'd brushed me. They seemed reddish, despite the blue of the water, and roughly the shape and size of the salmon I used to catch.

"Are there fish here?" I asked, wondering if I'd somehow missed them during all our other swims.

"Never." Summer had that flat, emotionless tone I recognized as her thinking voice. "Never here." Her eyes followed them under the ice. "I've never seen one anywhere unless it was at the end of a hook."

"Me neither," I added. Until this moment, I'd only seen squid below the surface. Fish had always been invisible until I'd caught them with a pole. Now, here they were—along with something else!

"Whoa, check out the plants!" My fist shot to the wavy green clumps growing along the river bottom. "These were definitely not here before."

Summer didn't reply, but bent down to try to scoop up a disintegrating handful.

In contrast to her even keel, I was positively beaming with excitement. "The world!" I exclaimed, realizing the bigger picture. "The world's gone through another change!"

Who knows when it had happened—probably sometime while we were in the Nether. It'd been about two weeks since we'd ventured outside the mountain. And in that time, for reasons we still couldn't understand, the world outside had spontaneously and miraculously transformed.

Now, if you've been in this world long enough to witness one of these changes, you know what I'm talking about. If not, try not to freak out, just like I did that first time, waking up and discovering that my left hand felt all tingly. Up until that point, I couldn't really use my left hand for much other than as an assistant to my right. After that moment, though, it could hold stuff independently—which was great! But that was just the start of the change.

On the downside, mobs were harder to kill. But on the up-side, I could now craft a shield to even the odds. I experienced another change later on, my boat suddenly appearing with oars when previously I'd had to lean forward to make it go. But that first change had been the most dramatic, and with it, I'd learned a valuable lesson: When the world changes, you've got to change with it. I can't stress how important that lesson was, and I think a lot of people have trouble with it back home.

Maybe I'm wrong, but I could vaguely remember our world always changing—new machines, new ways of doing stuff, new ideas—and how that change had really scared and angered a lot of people. Maybe they were worried about being left behind. Maybe they were just frustrated at having to relearn skills they thought they'd mastered. That had sure been the case in this world for me. But I did learn, and, as an added bonus, change taught me that I could adapt, that I shouldn't be afraid of it. When the world changes, you've got to change with it—'cause the world's gonna keep changing whether you want it to or not.

That's what was going through my mind now, taking in the fish and river grass.

"What else changed, do you think?" I asked, jumping out of the river and running up the bank.

I couldn't see any difference. No new animals or plants. Nothing but the same frosty nothingness. "Do you think it's just the water?" I asked. "*All* water? Should we hike to the coast, check the ocean?"

If the oceans had changed, what else could be out there? What would that mean for my island? "There's gotta be more on land," I mused, willing myself to see beyond the snow. "All that other land you told me about. All the places we're going to explore. We gotta get going! We gotta see!"

"We will," sighed Summer, holding up two pacifying arms, "after we finish lighting the mountain."

"What? But"—I fumbled through sleep-deprived adrenaline—"we've, like, already done so much. We've lit the kitchen, the chicken coops, my apartment—"

"Flat." Summer tried to correct. "The proper term is 'flat.'"

"Whatever," I bulldozed. "Point is, we got enough for all those, and the workshop and maybe, like, a couple storage closets."

"But not the main chamber."

"But that'll take forever!"

"But you promised."

I had. And although Summer's words felt as cold as the river, I couldn't deny that friends kept their promises. "You're right," I sighed, and looked up to the horizon.

"Guy." Summer's voice was softer now, warmer. "I know you want to pull up stakes this instant. I do, too. But it just wouldn't feel right not to finish what we started. And besides"—a tinge of verve in her voice—"you haven't seen the Ice Cube."

"Ice Cube?" I turned back, suddenly remembering the signpost. Our first day, down below, when I'd asked about it. She hadn't answered then and we hadn't talked about it since. One thing at a time. "Low-hanging fruit" first.

"I think you're up for it now," said Summer confidently. "Exploring a Nether fortress."

There were fortresses in the Nether?

"I've cleaned out a few of them," Summer continued, "and they're nowhere as easy as just picking glowstone in the wild." Summer got out of the river, walked down the bank, and, pick-axe in hand, began chipping away at the ice above the fish. "There's still one I haven't explored yet, and now I think you're ready to come with me." She paused over the open water, switching out her pickaxe for a regular axe. "Tomorrow, we'll head out to the Ice Cube."

She chopped.

I turned away, focusing on what she had in store for tomorrow.

A fortress. The Ice Cube. Clearly there were more Nether adventures I had to have before I could even think about moving on.

That night, after dinner and our standard pre-adventure prep, I did something I hadn't done in a very long time. I thought about the paintings on the wall.

I hadn't paid much attention to them in a while, even at first, when I'd been too overwhelmed by this whole new situation. That's why I'd given them only a passing mention in the earlier chapter, although their significance was practically shouting at me that night. They were the same ones from my house! The creeper, the man standing on the mountaintop, and the skinny-angular, videogame character of King Graham from the video-game *King's Quest*.

How was this possible? How could Summer and I have come up with the exact same images? Was this world choosing images for the canvas? Or were they buried memories? I'd bounced between both ideas, and I still wasn't any closer to either. If the pictures did come from the back of our minds, then it would mean Summer and I had lived pretty similar lives. That would explain the creeper—duh—but also the mountain man and King Graham. Could we have both seen them back on our world? And if that was the case, was it more than just coincidence?

The painting of King Graham seemed to take up most of my attention that night, and I'm not sure how long I stared at it before going to sleep. Why a computer game? And why such a simple one at that? I'd kinda had a breakthrough, back on my island, when I'd remembered that somehow computers were important to me. Maybe for a job, or for leisure, I couldn't be sure. But I knew they mattered, a lot, and if Summer's mind had conjured the exact same image, maybe they mattered to her as well.

"So many mysteries," I said, staring at Graham. "So many more questions to answer."

CHAPTER 13

One of those questions, a big one, was repeated in the dream I had that night. I hadn't dreamed in a while, or at least, I hadn't remembered them. Isn't that the case with dreams? You have them every night but don't remember most of them? I did with this one, parts of it anyway. The images were hazy, colorless. I was seated at a screen. Tapping away frantically and, I think, gliding another device across a flat surface. Was I working? Playing a game? Both?

I woke up even more anxious, even more curious than when I went to bed. One question was rising above the others, one that connected to both the dream and King Graham.

"Where do you think we are?" I asked Summer a few minutes into our trek. We were back in the Nether, heading in the opposite direction of our hunt for the small collection of glowstone. We were following the quartz-marked trail, on the watch for ghasts, heading to the fortress called the "Ice Cube."

"Eh?" Summer didn't seem very interested. Her mind was, as usual, focused on what was in front of us.

"Where do you think we are?" I continued speaking to her back. "This world, I mean? Do you think it's another planet? Another dimension?"

"Oh, that's easy," Summer replied, as easily as if I'd asked her how to craft a wooden shovel. "We're in a videogame."

I couldn't believe my ears. "You think?"

"Of course," Summer shrugged. "Haven't you had the dream?"

The words hit me like an invisible hammer. "Which one?"

She chuckled. "The screen-typing-computer one, of course."

"Ohmagod, yes!" I hopped next to her, bouncing with excitement. "Just last night! That's why I'm asking you now! I think I had that dream after looking at your paintings—our paintings, because I have some of the same ones back on my island."

"All the more reason for it to be a game." Summer's voice hinted at boredom. "How else could we come up with the same pictures? And it would explain everything else. The look of this landscape, up there and down here, and the physics of the world. Doesn't it all feel like a videogame to you?"

"Definitely," I started to answer, but with just a tad less enthusiasm. Something was knocking at the wall between the back and front of my mind. "But that's just a feeling."

"It has to be." Summer's tone was practical, inarguable. "Somehow we were pulled here, against our will, like that 'dude,' as you'd say, in the old movie you're always talking about where they fight with glowing Frisbees."

"Hm," I muttered, remembering the movie but forgetting the title.

"Or," Summer expanded, "we might have volunteered. Game testers, or designers. That could be us. We found some way to wipe our memories when we, I don't know, plugged our heads right into the system."

"Can we do that?" I asked. "Plug our heads into a computer?"

"No idea," sang Summer, "but if you can remember every piece of technology from the other world, do tell."

I couldn't. And I couldn't argue that the idea was sound. Game designers. Or testers. Or both. It did fit with our mutual dream. We're both sitting on some kind of laboratory beds back home, next to each other, or on opposite sides of the world, computers wired into helmets or, as Summer thought, directly into our heads. Ouch. The logic was sound, no doubt.

"But," I said, still wondering, "could the answer be something else?"

"Like what?" Summer challenged.

"Well . . ." I hesitated, unsure of my own gut. I thought about just agreeing with her and letting it go. We had a big day in front of us, and was an argument the best way to start it? But . . .

Friends aren't afraid to be honest with friends.

"What if it's a world, a real world, that's just made to look like a videogame for us."

"Eh?" Back home, a round, human Summer might have cocked her head. "How do you mean?"

"I've just been thinking," I began, "and I've thought about this a lot. What if this world was created for us . . . for people like us . . . to, well, learn stuff. Learn about ourselves, learn how to survive back in our world—"

"Why on earth would someone go and do that?" Summer balked. "And why on earth would it look like a videogame if it isn't one?"

"Simplicity?" I offered. "You know, the basic nature of it— less of everything from plants to animals to even the type of ground below us, or," I continued, glancing up, "above us on the surface. Not that much to figure out, when you think about it, which gives us more time to think about ourselves."

"But why the videogame look?" countered Summer. "The whole blockiness of everything. Why make it look and feel like we're in a videogame instead of creating just a simulation of our world with, as you say, less of everything?"

"I've thought about that too," I continued, which got a sarcastic "Now that's a surprise" in return.

"No, hear me out," I said with growing confidence. "Did you play videogames back home?"

"Definitely."

"A lot?"

"Definitely."

"Me too. In fact, I think it's kinda like a common language back home. Like eating or music, or maybe sports." I couldn't remember if I ever played sports, but that didn't matter right now. "What if whoever designed this world did it in a way that we, castaways like you and me, can re-create later in our world?"

"Agaaain"—Summer stretched the word—"why, in either world, would someone want to do that?"

"As a teaching tool," I breathed, really getting into the swing of my thoughts. "A life-lesson teaching tool wrapped up in a fun game."

Summer was silent for a moment, no doubt accepting the mind-blowing power of my insight.

It made so much sense. It couldn't be anything else. A world created to teach us how to be a better version of ourselves, which we could then re-create on computers for everyone else to play. How simple. How perfect. In the few seconds it took Summer to answer, I pictured myself as one of those historical figures from long ago. You know, the kind wrapped in a sheet sitting on a rock while other sheet-clad dudes sat at his feet saying, "Ah, you are a genius, please tell us more!"

"No," Summer responded flatly. "You're wrong. It's a video-game."

"You don't know that."

"It has to be."

"But you don't know!"

"Neither do you."

"But I will!" I declared, wishing I could shake my finger in the air. "When we escape, when we leave this world for ours, I'll be able to prove that I'm right!"

"And until that day," Summer chimed back, "we'll both have to just respect each other's beliefs!"

"Respect each other's beliefs," I repeated, mentally checking off another friendship lesson. But that fresson suddenly took a backseat to my shout of "Whoa!"

I stopped in my tracks, forcing a huffing halt from Summer. "What now?"

"Do you know what you just said?" I asked.

"Something that won't delay our mission, I hope?" Summer quipped.

"You know . . ." I grasped for the thought, as elusive as an attacking ghost. "I think you just summed up a really important lesson about our world!"

"Here it comes," Summer sighed.

"No, really." I waved my arms. "I think what you said about respecting each other's beliefs, a belief you can't prove until you cross from one world to the next . . . I think"—I exhaled deeply—"folks back home don't do that, or don't do it enough. In fact, I think that some believe what they believe so violently that they're actually willing to kill each other over it."

"You really think so?" Summer asked. "You think people back home are that mad?"

"I'm not so sure," I said, head swimming with ideas. "But I think I remember something like that from back home. Don't you?"

"I try not to think too much about back home." Summer shrugged, which should have prompted an entirely new, and really critical, conversation. Summer tried not to think about back home? Why?

That's what I should have asked next, if I hadn't been so caught up in high-minded notions about beliefs.

"I think . . ." I continued.

"You certainly do," sniped Summer, turning to continue our

hike, "and when we get back to the mountain, you can think and ponder and philosophize all you blo—"

She stopped. Words and motion. She was a couple dozen steps ahead, frozen at the top of a small rise.

FLP.

The sound answered my unasked question.

It was coming from beyond her, somewhere on the other side.

FLP-FLP-FLP.

A mushy, squishy sound getting closer by the second.

I rushed up next to Summer, scanning the rusty, uniform landscape before us.

"There." Summer pointed to a distant cube that appeared larger and darker than the rest. And crooked.

Crooked?

I was about to ask what I was looking at when the crooked cube moved. Not far, not fast—just a short, shallow hop in our direction. And on the second hop, I could make out what looked like eyes.

"Magma cube," said Summer. "The Nether's version of a slime."

Slime?

I thought I might have skimmed over a passage about slime in my island's monster manual. But if they were a real threat, I'm sure I would have read deeper.

And as if to complement that thought, Summer continued, "Not very dangerous, not like ghasts, but this one is in our way."

"I'll handle it," I boasted, reaching for my sword. She might dismiss my philosophical revelations, but she couldn't dispute my warrior skills.

"If you wish," said Summer, "even though it might be safer with a bow."

"You're worried about safety?" I snorted. "With that bopping bag o' jelly?"

"Oh, by all means," Summer giggled, "save the day."

I hesitated. "What's the matter?"

"No, nothing"—Summer stifled another giggle—"unless you'd like a little help?"

"Puh-lease," I sneered. "I got this."

Can't be too dangerous, I thought, striding purposefully across the crunchy, speckled ground. *I mean, if I can take a ghast, what can this dopey hop-rock do?*

The "hop-rock" must have seen me coming, because its next bounce brought those eyes level with mine. "Come on then," I said, trying to imitate Summer's accent. "Give it a go."

I stepped forward to swing just as the magma cube bounced . . . right on top of me!

"OW!" I yelped, reeling from the burning impact. Honestly, it wasn't too bad, no different than a zombie's punch. But the blow to my pride, especially when I knew I had an audience, was enough to send my sword to work.

"Ha!" I yelled, as the diamond blade sliced through living lava. The cube flashed red, falling back in silent pain.

Rushing forward for a second, hopefully fatal blow, I shouted over my shoulder, "No problem!"

The blade connected, but the creature didn't die. Instead, it split into four—no fooling, four!—smaller versions of itself.

"'No problem!'" called Summer, as the hopping quartet attacked.

"Eee!" I squealed, getting knocked and burned by the cubes as I swiped wildly around with my sword.

"You got this?" asked Summer with a slightly more serious tone.

"I got this!" I insisted as the blade swished a sweeping slice across all four cubes.

"About . . ." I began, but bit down on "time." They'd split again! Four into eight!

Hop-bounce-burn!

Surrounding me, pouncing.

"Ow-jee-aw, c'mon!"

A well-placed chop turned one into smoke.

At least they stop dividing at this level.

Two more at my back, another three on either side. Leaping for my face, searing through my armor.

I got this! I kept repeating to myself through swipes and singes. *I got this!*

Bouncing and burning. So many, too many. What was that movie I'd seen once, that phrase that had been funny *then* . . .

I got it, I got it, I got . . . I AIN'T GOT IT!

"Summer! I need—"

"Help," said the calm voice behind me. "I figured you would."

Another blade at my side, dicing the . . . living dice. "You go right, I'll go left." The feeling of Summer's shoulder against mine. Comforting, secure. A minute or so later, we were standing in silence with a few red and yellow balls hovering at our feet.

"Magma cream," said Summer, swiping up the first of two. "The prime ingredient for fireproof potions."

"You know, Summer," I said, as hyper-healing fixed everything but my pride, "I wasn't calling you 'cause I needed help or anything. I just thought, like, you shouldn't be missing all the fun."

"Of course." Summer handed me a ball of magma cream. "And just so you know, in the future, there's nothing wrong with asking for help."

Fresson fifteen: Friends shouldn't be afraid to ask friends for help.

"Onward then." Summer led us back onto the quartz trail, down into a narrow, flat ditch. Here we had limited visibility, and I noticed Summer swinging her bow back and forth.

"We should probably fill this in tomorrow," she said, looking up and listening for ghasts. "It'll make the final stretch to the Ice Cube easier to see."

"Why do you call it the Ice Cube?" I asked. "Is it the color?"

"And the mod-cons," Summer answered, "which you will definitely thank me for building."

"You built it?" I asked, now thoroughly confused. "I thought it was the fortress we were going to explore."

"Dear me, no." Summer chuckled. "That's my forward base, so to speak—my home away from home. A place to restock, catch our breath in safety, and, above all, cool down."

"Say what?" I couldn't have heard that right. "You mean, like, emotionally cool down, not physically change your temperature."

"Not at all," said Summer as the terrain began to rise. "I

couldn't manage these deep-range missions if I didn't have a place to cool down. Overheating saps too much strength, clouds thinking. I've made too many mistakes down here, lots of them life-threatening, to not appreciate the importance of beating the heat."

"I get what you're saying, but how did you—"

"With that."

As we crested the ridge, Summer gestured ahead. "Behold the Ice Cube."

CHAPTER 14

A large structure, stark white against the bruised plum backdrop. It couldn't have been more alien or beautiful to my dry, blinking eyes.

"The Ice Cube?" I asked.

Summer nodded, and started toward the aptly named box.

"Quartz?" was my next question, which got me another nod. "Easy to spot, even without night vision." And, on cue, our potions faded and our eyes returned to normal. Even in the haze, it shone as clearly as a lighthouse in ocean fog.

As we continued across the crunching heat, Summer explained, "Took quite a bit of time, I can tell you, and while it's not exactly ghost-proof, the outer wall is easy enough to repair."

Outer wall? Mentally, I braced for what had to be another eye-popping tour. I could already spot Summer's signature retractable gravel slits, and as we approached the wooden front door, she explained that "I would have preferred iron, but the open holes would let all the cool air escape."

"Cool air." I shook my head. "Why am I surprised that I'm surprised?"

Summer laughed, opened the door, and ushered me into a dark vestibule, then reached up to switch on the redstone lamps above us.

"Oh," I moaned, embraced by a welcome wash of arctic air. "Whoa boy."

Summer chuckled again, motioning all around us. "Three walls: quartz outside and quartz inside, with packed snow in the middle."

"You brought snow from up top." I leaned my face against the chilled quartz wall.

"It doesn't melt," said Summer, "even when exposed to the air." I saw her looking up and did the same. Checkerboarded amidst the redstone lamps were iron grates, and behind their bars, cubes of frozen flaked water.

"Simple thermodynamics," chirped Summer. "Hot air rises, cold air descends."

"Oh yeah"—I gave an exaggerated nod—"simple, you just invented air-conditioning." I motioned to the next door. "And through there is, what, the car-boat-jetfighter that looks like a bat?"

Summer laughed so hard she bumped her shoulder against mine. "Oh, Guy."

No, there wasn't a superhero lair beyond this temperature-controlled "airlock," but the main room did have supply chests, raised beds of potatoes, and a jukebox playing one of those weird musical discs I have yet to acquire a taste for. Still, I couldn't help but marvel at all the time and effort that had gone into this home away from home.

"What's that?" I asked, pointing to what looked like a four-legged iron box full of water in the corner.

"A cauldron," answered Summer, filling three of her empty bottles from the little cube. "Only way to store water in the Nether. For some reason it instantly evaporates, even in here, if you pour it onto the ground."

"So, water doesn't make water down here," I mused as Summer handed me a drink.

"A bit of an inconvenience," she replied, refilling the cauldron with a full bucket from her pack, "all this BYOW nonsense. Still"—she gestured to our luxurious surroundings—"I think it's worth it, don't you?"

"Mhm!" My mind was already spinning after I'd finished chugging the throat-quenching bottle. But then, because my head was tilted toward the ceiling, I saw something that instantly re-dried my throat.

"Summer." I hesitated, scrounging for diplomatic words. "I count almost a hundred redstone lamps . . . I mean . . . minus the six . . . eight spaces you've got for AC vents . . ."

I let my words trail off, not sure exactly how to finish the thought.

"Yes?" Summer asked with the slightest edge to her voice. "And your point is?"

I didn't even know why I was so nervous. I mean, it was just an honest question.

"Well . . . wouldn't it be easier to just use these lamps, and the ones in the vestibule, and all the glowstone we've harvested to finish lighting the mountain?"

A pause, so slight it probably lasted less than half a second. But to me, that tense waiting . . .

Where's a good ghast attack when you need one?

"Oh, yes," Summer replied coolly. "I can see how you'd think that way. I did too, actually, when I considered building this place." She nodded emphatically, then downed her bottle of water. "But this is just a fraction of what we'll eventually need and"—maybe this was my imagination, but I could almost feel her voice relaxing with each word—"yes, we'll be taking it with us when we finally pack it all in, but until then, we'll need this place to rest and cool down. Especially," she said, her voice picking up in excitement as she sauntered over to a lever next to the far wall, "when our next stop is this!"

FLK.

The gravel dropped before the glass windows.

"Dang." I was staring out across another ocean of lava, topped by something straight out of a fantasy adventure novel.

A black fortress rising out of the molten rock. Thin, sinister towers connected by narrow bridges that made my head swim.

"I haven't explored this one yet," she admitted, "but if it's anything like the other two I've cleaned out, then those halls are crawling with some truly nasty brutes. Blazes and wither skeletons that make surface mobs look like harmless snow bunnies. But once we get past them to there"—she gestured toward the far end of the fortress, to all the glowstone deposits hanging just above it—"and with us working as a team, we'll have more than we need in no time at all!" Her voice was so cheery, so optimistic. At that moment, I couldn't even remember why I'd brought up the Ice Cube's lamps in the first place.

"Trust me, Guy."

Friends trust each other.

"I do."

After a quick fist bump, and armed with more water and another dose of night vision, we exited the Ice Cube into that infernal body slam of heat.

"Never thought I'd identify with the upper deck of a furnace," I mumbled.

"What was that?" Summer asked, bow and eyes scanning the sky.

"Nothing," I replied, not wanting to seem like a complainer. "How are we gonna get over there?"

I couldn't see any connection between our cliff and the fortress. Which I guess makes sense for why it was there. I mean, if the whole point of a fortress is defense, what's more defensible than an ocean-sized moat of flames?

Summer didn't seem bothered, though. "This way." She pointed down the cliff's edge.

I couldn't see what she was directing me to at first, confused by the feature-obscuring netherrack. I leaned over to peer closer. "Careful!" Summer tried to dart in front of me. "Mind the gap!"

I did. Not far, just a few blocks down onto a staircase. It was dug right into the ground, and angled in such a way that I'd totally missed it.

"I meant to do that," I said, looking up at her.

"Of course you did." Summer landed gracefully next to me, then stepped in front.

"Onward," Summer chirped, and disappeared.

We came out just at the shore of the lava, close enough to feel it bake every exposed patch of skin.

"You invent a fireproof boat?" I half-joked, backing up as far as I could.

"No need," Summer answered seriously, motioning down the "beach" to a strip of land—I think the word is "isthmus"—that connected to the closest tower.

At first, I was relieved that it was both wide and at sea level—well, lava level. But when we got closer, I saw that the material was darker, browner, and finer than the ever-present netherrack.

"Soul sand," remarked Summer, "which, trust me, you do not want to tread upon."

"Is it quick?" I asked. "You know, like that stuff back home that's supposed to swallow you whole?"

"Quite the opposite," explained Summer, as we stepped right up to the woody-colored grains. "It holds you in place, slows you down. A nuisance in the best of times, but in a battle . . ."

"I got it," I nodded, staring closer at what appeared to be ominous faces in the sand. Maybe I was imagining that, though. I looked over at Summer and watched her remove stacked netherrack from her pack. "Want me to keep an eye on the sky?"

"You got it." She nodded, and went to work covering the soul sand. I kept watch, bow in hand, waiting for those creepy floating squid-balloons. It was tense going, eyes darting this way and that for anything that looked out of the ordinary—as if that word had any meaning anymore—and straining my ears for that nightmarish screaming.

But the floating bombers never came, and in a few short,

sweat-evaporating minutes, Summer had built a bridge all the way to the tower.

"Now"—a diamond pickaxe glinted in her hand—"we do what we do best."

And we dug. Taking turns, cracking through a dark, tough substance that Summer identified as "nether bricks." This phase actually frazzled me more than crossing the isthmus, because, if you remember, we were tunneling blind through a pillar surrounded by lava. One mistake, one nether brick too many and . . . well, you can picture the results. I sure did. And when we finally broke into open air, I breathed a dry, lung-baking sigh of relief.

"About ruddy time," puffed Summer, leading me up onto what must have once been an intersection. The roofless structure was composed of four connected doorways, three of which led nowhere. The fourth, however, opened onto one of those connecting bridges I'd seen from the Ice Cube. I think the technical term is "catwalk," which I guess comes from the idea that only a cat would be crazy enough to cross one. Three blocks wide. That's all we had, with an extra one-block raised guard on either side. No rail. No fence. And, unlike a cat, no nine lives.

Summer was beside me now, bow ready. "From here we can get a good sense of where to start building our 'stairways to heaven.'"

I didn't get the reference. And I didn't have time to ask about it.

"You got your fireproof potion handy?" Summer asked, scanning the pink mist.

"No, but . . ." I started to say, then heard a new noise. It was a muffled, distant THF-THF-THF, and Summer shouted, "Look out!" before shoving me up against a protective corner between two doorways.

"Drink your potion!" she ordered as three fireballs streaked past us. These weren't ghast missiles. They were smaller, faster. I watched them strike the nether bricks behind us with just enough force to set them alight.

"Stay here!" Summer commanded, then leapt to the safety of the opposite corner. "It's right out there."

"What?!" I squeaked, and peeked out from behind the barrier.

It was smaller than a ghast, golden and smoking. A humanoid head perched atop rotating rods. It didn't seem to make any sound . . . that is, until it launched another tri-flame. That was the THF-THF-THF sound that had made me pull my head in like a turtle.

"It's a blaze," said Summer. "They come from spawners in the fortress, and the longer we delay attacking, the more chance of its gathering more mates."

"Let me draw its fire," I suggested, surprised at my courage. "You've gotta have more experience hitting those things at a distance."

"Good point," Summer agreed, nocking an arrow to her bow, "but for Pete's sake, be careful on that catwalk!"

I didn't know who Pete was, but I got the message loud and clear.

"Here I am!" I shouted, running out into the open. "Here's your target!"

THF-THF-THF. Three shots, right behind me, close enough to burn my backside.

"Too slow!" I shot back, turning to face it.

THF-THF-THF. Right at me, but slow enough to dodge.

"Ha!" I taunted, evading more incendiary rounds. "Gotta try harder!"

WHP! Summer's arrow streaked from the tower's doorway, barely missing the bobbing blaze. "Almost had it!" called Summer. "Keep it distracted."

"No problem!" I replied, realizing how helpful all those ghast battles had been.

Just like with anticipating where those sky-squids would be, I'd mastered the art of calling their shots as well. Blaze strikes might have been a little bit faster, but the principle was still the same. It didn't take too much adjustment to dance out of their way.

You heard me: "dance." My signature victory spin-hop.

"And you may find yourself in a giant subterranean oven!" I sang, rewriting a barely remembered song that'd floated through my mind since my time on the island.

THF-THF-THF. Break left.

"And you might find yourself in a fantasy fortress facing a gold-y, float-y, fire thing!"

THF-THF-THF. Break right.

"And you might ask yourself, well, how did I ge—aaahhh!"

Big mistake! I was so distracted with making up my song that I'd stepped on a burning square of nether brick. I'd observed that, unlike netherrack, its darker, denser cousin only burned for a few seconds when lit. What I didn't take the time to confirm, however, was exactly how many seconds I had.

A lesson from my time on the island leapt to the front of my mind. *Details make the difference.*

"Yaaaaa!" I howled as flames rose up before my eyes.

Pain.

Panic!

I ran for what I thought was the safety of the tower.

"STOP!" cried Summer, halting my flaming feet.

I was right on the edge of the "guard." One more step and . . .

"Here!" A voice to guide me, calm me. "This way, Guy!"

Following my crisping ears, I made it to the corner.

"Stay still!" A few more eternal seconds before the torturous flames finally burned away.

Vision clearing, eyes regenerating. Summer yelling at me from the far corner.

"Didn't you take your fireproof potion?"

"Uh . . ."

"No matter." She raised her bow for another shot. "Just pop a healer!"

The bottle in my belt, in my hands, and then the salty sting of instant health.

"Lemme get back out there!" I offered, ready to rejoin the fray.

"No need!" Summer wasn't mad, just focused. I watched the arrow leave her bow, then peeked out just in time to see our foe drift away in a puff of smoke.

"Pity." Summer was looking down now, watching the remaining blaze rod fall slowly into the lava below. "Can always use one of those." She turned to me, adding, "Still, plenty more when we find the spawner. Let's go!"

CHAPTER 15

Summer's eyes swept the fortress. "One of them has to be close."

I nodded, trying to listen, as my eyes followed the falling blaze rod.

That could have been me.

Just like with the magma cube, I'd allowed myself to get over-confident.

"Off we go," trumpeted Summer, trotting down the nether brick road.

Trailing in her wake, I tried to keep track of all our threats. Ghasts, blazes, one wrong step over the guard . . .

It was all I could do to keep focused, to not be distracted by the sheer complexity of this towered labyrinth before us. How had she done it? Conquered two of them all by herself? Just that fact alone gave me the confidence to follow her every step.

THF-THF-THF!

"On the left!"

At her warning I stopped short, as the three flares passed between us.

Smoke! Out of the corner of my eye.

THF-THF-THF! I sidestepped this time, bringing around my bow.

"Don't shoot!" I paused in confusion as Summer beat it for the intersection. "We'll lose the blaze rod if we don't lead it over solid ground!"

I followed, then halted abruptly as another volley crossed our path. Then we were off again, stopping at the intersection, turning to fight as the spinning hunter hovered up and onto the catwalk.

Summer shouted, "Now!" Her sword glinted in the gloom. "No more wasting arrows!"

"Are you . . ." I don't know if the last word would have been "kidding," "serious," or "crazy," but none of them had come out before she charged our enemy.

"C'mon, Guy!" she called over her shoulder. "We've got 'im!"

What a sight, even from my running, shaky vantage point. Summer the Slayer, with courage born of endless experience. She dodged and weaved, and then, when she was just underneath it, gave a high, slicing leap! Her blade struck with a less-than-dramatic CLINK, and in two follow-up strokes, it was all over. I gave a whooping cheer for her performance.

"Thank you!" Summer emerged from the dissipating smoke with a yellowish orange stick. "One blaze rod to go."

"That's what powers the brewing stand?" I asked.

"And can be turned into blaze powder for strength potions," she answered, stowing the rod in her pack. "And there's plenty more where that came from."

Summer motioned to another structure farther down the catwalk. Unlike the open "doorway" towers, this column was capped with an enclosed structure. I could see barred windows and a fenced-off roof. I could also see that the roof nearly scraped the cavern ceiling, and that something was flickering in the narrow, open space.

"There's the spawner," Summer announced, and took off with me in tow.

Don't spawn, I silently prayed as we ran in the opposite direction of safety, *please don't make any more of those . . .*

No such luck.

With roughly twenty blocks to go, I saw the flaming little cage breathe a blaze to life.

"Faster!" cried Summer, darting into the empty structure below it. It was some kind of garden, with two rows of soul sand sprouting large, red mushrooms—different from what I'd seen on the surface.

I didn't have time to examine them, or even ask what they were. Our goal was the staircase that rose between the two plots, and the newly spawned blaze that waited at the top.

This time, Summer didn't charge. She waited for a moment at the first step. I could see her eyes darting across the dark purple roof. Was she trying to locate our target by sound?

I'd thought blazes were completely quiet, but soon realized I just hadn't been close enough to hear them breathe. It was a really creepy sound: slow, labored, and slightly metallic, like someone trying to suck air through a pipe.

"Hhhuh-hhhoh-hhhuh-hhhoh."

"Still just one," she noted calmly, eyes lowering to the stairs, "and if it won't come to us . . ."

Off again, bounding up the stairs with a cry of "Keep up!"

"Can't wait!" I huffed sourly, bursting onto the roof just as a rotating fiend turned toward us.

THF-THF-THF!

Summer and I parted quickly, giving the fireballs a wide berth.

"Quickly!" she shouted, racing for the blaze. "Before it gets away."

I think she meant hover off the roof and out of sword range. I personally wouldn't have minded its getting away, especially before another blaze puffed into existence. But I didn't argue or hesitate. The impact off my blade sounded, and felt, like I was striking metal. I could feel the hard crack reverberate through my hand.

A few short blows from both of us was all it took to give that blaze the blues.

Okay, so maybe I still need to work on my wit, but you get it. We took it down so quickly and easily that I had more than enough time to turn my attention to the spawner.

"No, wait!" Summer's words caught my pickaxe mid-swing. "Don't destroy it!" She held out a handful of netherrack. "Just seal it in. Hurry!"

Urgently, she began blocking up the narrow space between

the roof's fence and the overhanging land. I followed suit, asking, "What could we possibly gain by—"

Another tortured "Hhuh-hhhoh," with Summer and me only halfway done. I turned to face a newly spawned blaze.

"Summer!"

"I know!"

Her blade had already fallen, making her the burner's target. I reached for my sword and accidentally pulled out my pickaxe, but saw that I didn't have time to switch. Summer leapt sideways as sparking triplets hit the fence behind her. I struck, hard and fast. Summer followed with a frontal assault. The blaze let out a final, groaning gasp, then vanished into a smoking rod.

"Finish the job!" Summer swiped up the rod and ran back to seal up the spawner. I continued on my end, counting the seconds until another blaze showed. Luckily, by the time we heard the breath of a new, living blowtorch, Summer was fixing the last netherrack block to the staircase.

"Right then!" She gave a long, deep sigh, then preempted my question with: "I know what you're thinking: Isn't it dangerous leaving that monster maker up and running? But blaze rods are what power brewing stands." I remained silent, so she followed up with, "So even when we leave the Nether, we'll still be able to come here to get more for potions."

It made sense, in the moment. But I'm sure if I had really thought about it, as I did much, much later, I might have wondered if it actually made more sense to just stock up on enough obsidian to make portals to visit the Nether for whatever we needed when we needed it later, after we were on the move.

But I wasn't really thinking about it. And unlike my previous, solo life on the island, when any time was a good time for a mental puzzle break, I was still junior partner in a mission that was nowhere near over.

So, with a trusting "Okay," I followed her back down the stairs and into the dark passage beyond. "Don't bother with the nether wart," she said, gesturing to the garden.

So that's what nether wart looks like.

"I grow them up top. And besides"—she hesitated at the hall's entrance—"too many other goodies stashed about."

Just then my night vision began to wink out.

"Uh, Summer . . ."

"Me too," she answered, reaching for another bottle. "Time to top off."

I did likewise, noticing my dwindling inventory. "One left after this."

"All we'll need," she declared, striding confidently into the corridor. "One glowstone harvest, and maybe a few bonus goodies, and we'll be on our way."

She stopped at the first intersection, turning back the way we came. "But first . . ."

I watched her take a crafting table from her belt, place it on the floor, then whip up a signpost marked "Home."

"Just in case we lose our way."

She really knows what she's doing, I thought, following her farther down the passageway and down another flight of stairs. I noticed that the barred windows here looked out onto solid netherrack, and when I asked if we were underground, Summer explained that parts of these fortresses were embedded in the surrounding land.

"Easier to get lost," she said, placing another signpost, "but at least you don't have to worry about ghosts and blazes."

Summer was a few steps ahead of me by then, turning right around a corner.

I heard an exultant "A-ha!" and a second later, saw the reason why.

Farther down the hall, just before another turn, was a standard storage box that seemed as out of place as us.

"Fancy some treasure?" she asked, and bounded forward with a lighthearted skip.

Treasure! So that's what she'd meant by "bonus goodies."

And they were!

Summer pulled out a handful of gold ingots, then a pair of sparkling diamonds.

"Whoa," I breathed, then asked, "Can you mine gold and diamonds down here?"

"Not that I've found," answered Summer, which, naturally, got my mind working overtime on the big "Why?"

Why were they here? Already mined and processed and placed in these chests? Who did that? And for that matter, who built these fortresses to begin with? Like the mine under my island, had they been constructed by a long-extinct civilization? What had happened to them? Were they turned into zombie pigmen?

"Ever seen these?" Summer raised a coat of diamond armor in one hand, and what looked like a leather saddle in the other.

"I have!" I said, recognizing it as belonging to an animal. "At least the armor. I found that on my island. And I read about the saddle in a guidebook. They're for horses, right? Or pigs? Have you ever seen a horse or a pig?"

"Both," said Summer, pocketing the armor, "and donkeys, and even ocelots when I've been to the jungle."

"Have you ever ridden one?" I asked. "A horse? Or even a pig?" My mind filled with images of Summer galloping across the snow astride her trusty war swine.

"Not yet," she answered, still rummaging through the chest. "Haven't had the chance."

"Well, there'll be plenty of chances," I said confidently, "when we continue our journey!"

Summer didn't answer, but instead held up a sword of pure gold. "Here"—she handed me the shining blade—"you should have this."

"Nice!" Standing back, I gave the blade a few practice swipes. "Thanks!" It wasn't the sword itself—I could have made a dozen back on my island. But since gold was inferior to diamonds in both luster and strength, I kept the rare yellow metal for other things. It was the excitement of finding it, the idea that these dark, menacing structures could hold pleasant surprises, that grabbed me.

Summer must have sensed my enthusiasm. "Enjoying yourself?"

"You know it! Who knew this place could be so much fun?"

CLICK-CLICK.

Sounds, farther up the passageway.

CLICK-SHCLICK.

Bones. Skeletons! I could tag that sound in my sleep. But

these were different somehow. Flatter, scraping, as if bones were being dragged across the hard brick floor.

"Wither skeletons," said Summer, closing the chest.

Shclick-shclick.

"Bring 'em on." I reached for my diamond sword.

"Mm-mm," Summer intoned, shaking her head violently. "Trust me, you do NOT want to get close enough to be touched."

Just then, a figure clacked around the corner.

It looked like a skeleton, but it was black as newly mined coal. And instead of a bow it carried a sword made from common gray stone.

"So that's a wither skeleton?" I asked.

"In the nonflesh," Summer replied. Her bow was up, an arrow nocked to shoot. "I'll do this one." She loosed a shaft into its midnight skull.

The ebony frame flashed red, hopped back a step, then clacked toward us with stone sword ready.

"Your turn. I'd recommend keeping your distance," said Summer, stepping aside to let me shoot. But my bow wasn't ready. I was still armed only with my sword. "Never mind—two more!"

Behind the first skeleton. Summer shot one of them, then shot it again, and a leg bone dropped amid a puff of smoke.

"I got it!" I said. I'd used my sword, but now switched to my bow. I lined up the original skeleton and shot without fully drawing back the string. The result was a hit that probably didn't do too much damage. But the impact did knock it back. As I lined up to finish it off, Summer loosed three arrows quickly on the third skeleton.

Five arrows hit within four seconds. And all before our attackers could get anywhere near us.

"That's it?" I said, scooping up the three dropped femurs — or lemurs? Whatever the medical term for leg bones are. "That easy?"

"Unless they touch you," said Summer, continuing up the empty hall, "and give you a pinch of 'wither.'"

"Can't be any worse than spider's poison," I snorted.

"It is." Summer's voice was low, serious, and no doubt packed with memory. "Much worse."

She didn't elaborate. I didn't press. Especially when I saw her pick up her pace. There was another staircase in front of us, and something was glowing up at the top.

Just like the blaze spawner tower, this room was pressed right up against the netherrack ceiling. But instead of a smoldering monster factory, this roof was practically tiled with glowstone!

"Jackpot!" I cried, and turned to my nodding partner.

There must have been at least two dozen blocks, and between the two of us, we hacked and smashed and shattered it all out within minutes.

"So much!" I said, gathering the last pinch of yellow dust. "And all in one place!"

"Quite," replied Summer with just a tad less enthusiasm. "But the problem with glowstone is that you lose some dust every time you smash one."

"Yeah, but you gotta admit," I countered, "that this is still a heck of a . . . haul." I yawned the last word, which gave my partner a chance to chuckle.

"You need a rest," she said sympathetically. "We both do."

She started heading back down the stairs. "Let's get up to the surface, have a good night's sleep, and then come right back here tomorrow for another haul."

"Now yer"—a brief yawn—"talkin'."

Following her signs, we trotted back down the corridor, past the blocked-up spawner, then down our tower staircase and across the covered soul sand isthmus.

As we ascended the netherrack stairs through the cliff, the ethereal wail of a ghast floated down.

"Don't," warned Summer, motioning to my bow, "we're too hot and tired. Best to just pop into the Ice Cube for a bit, have a water, and cool down, and then if it's still knocking about we'll be in much better shape for combat."

"Makes sense," I said, trying to stifle another yawn.

And as if it were part of our conversation, the overhead ghast gave another cry. "Brehhh!"

Summer downed a speed potion. "No need to be stingy now." Then waited for me to do the same.

With me barely a block behind her, we dashed up the remaining steps. There it was: the Ice Cube in front of us, with a screeching ghast behind.

I heard the launch, felt the impact through my feet, the heat at my back. Just a few more steps.

"Brehhh!"

Too slow. No match for adrenaline and bottled speed.

The door behind me. Slamming shut. Cool, refreshing air. The second door. Bright light. Security.

Summer lowered the gravel windows to observe our foiled attacker. It was hovering over the cliff, barely ten yards from our window. But just like so many other mobs, it seemed to lose interest once we were behind glass.

"Good call," I said, taking a long, quenching gulp of water.

"Mm," Summer mumbled as she downed her own drink. "Now you see the need for a forward base."

"You think of . . ." I mumbled, then yawned "everything," as all my tension drained away.

How long had it been since we'd slept? A night? Maybe two? I'd forgotten what real sleep deprivation could do to my body, and my mind.

I wasn't thinking straight. But that's no excuse for what happened next.

"You know," I said, reaching into my pack, "who needs to head back up to the surface when we can catch a few z's right here?"

The bed was in my hand, expanding to a spot on the floor.

Summer raised her hands to stop me. Too late. I started to slide into the bed right as I heard her yell, "NOOOO!"

CHAPTER 16

We've all seen this moment in movies, many times. Something is about to happen, something terrible, with someone trying, in slow motion, to stop it. Heroes running toward their comrades to save them, or away from the flames of an exploding building. Everything slowed down, with tense, atmospheric music playing in the background, as you wait to see if they'll make it in time.

I think it had been done so many times that now it was actually something to make fun of. I can recall seeing parodies, commercials, and cartoons, and even laughing out loud at some of them.

But now it was happening to me, and I wasn't laughing. I got to the bed, while, out of the corner of my eye, I could see Summer across the room, hyper-reaching to place something in front of me. A block. Netherrack. Just as I reached over it for the bed.

The world flashed white.

Blind, deaf. The blast lifting me off my feet.

Up and back, slamming hard into the rear wall. Choking, stunned. Hyper-healing. Pain.

I hit the floor, facedown. I called for Summer, coughed, tried to blink through regenerating eyes, then felt something pushed into the thrashed wreck of my hand. A bottle!

Stinging lips parted, opening my throat. The ache of fizzing liquid. Watermelon. Instant health!

"S-s-summer?" I croaked through mending vocal cords. "Summer?!"

Darkness became shapes, which sharpened into clarity. I could see again. There she was! Not standing over me as I expected, but racing away, toward the wreckage.

The Ice Cube. Ruined!

At least that's how it looked at first glance. As I rose, hacked, and blinked in more of my surroundings, I could see that only a corner was destroyed, and only the first two layers. One last wall remained, one thin barrier of quartz between us and the hovering ghast. If that hadn't been the case, if we'd been open to its missiles while still recovering from the blast . . .

"Summer," I heaved, stumbling clumsily toward her. "I'm so sorry."

"It's all right." Summer didn't turn to face me. I could see that she was frantically gathering up hovering blocks, shoving them into storage chests as quickly as she could swipe them off the floor. I could also see that a lot of the blocks weren't just wall debris. The exploding bed must have taken out one of her storage chests as well.

"Oh my God, Summer," I said, as the ringing in my ears subsided, "I'm so sorry I forgot about the exploding bed!"

"It's all right," she repeated tersely. "Just rest a bit—don't move or speak."

"I . . ." I didn't know what to say. I felt so horribly guilty. Instinctively I wobbled closer to the wreckage. "Here"—I reached for a floating stack of snowballs—"let me help . . ."

"No, no," snapped Summer, moving between me and the rubble. "Leave it with me. Just rest for a bit, rest." She didn't seem angry, just . . . what's the word? Rushed? Nervous?

And why shouldn't she have been? Don't dropped items in this world have a shelf life? Don't they vanish if you don't pick them up right away? All her precious building materials, all her meticulously stored items!

"I can help you," I said, trying to get past her to the mess. "Seriously, let me help you."

"I don't need your help," she snapped, throwing something into a nearby chest. "You need to take care of your wounds."

"But you're wounded too!" I said, now doubly guilty that she'd almost died saving me. "If you don't heal . . ."

She pushed in front of me as I spoke, grabbing another pile of something.

I looked down to see that there were identical piles of that same something. A lot of piles. Bright. Yellow.

"Summer?" I began, knowing the answer. "What is that?"

"Nothing," she responded, knowing the answer as well.

"Summer." Stomach tightening, skin sweating in the cold air. "That's glowstone."

"Not really." Her voice was high, her words quick. "Not much."

So much.

I didn't have to do the arithmetic to guess how much.

"Summer." Now my voice was deeper, more confident. "That looks like more than enough to . . ."

"No, no, no, no . . ." She still wouldn't look at me, frantically scooping up the hovering truth. "You don't understand."

I didn't.

I couldn't wrap my square brain around what was happening.

All this time. All the glowstone harvesting we'd been doing. It was already here. Ready to go. Why?!

"You really don't understand," Summer repeated, dumping the last pile into another chest. "It's not enough. Really."

"Can I look?" I don't know where my words came from. "Can I count?" Don't get me wrong. I was just as terrified as I'd been with the chickens. Even more so, because as scary as it was to reveal something to Summer, it was even scarier to have her reveal something to me. "If that's not enough, can I count it for myself?"

"No." Summer turned to face me, moving her body between me and the chest. "You don't have to. I know what I'm talking about. Just trust me, all right? Trust me."

But I didn't. And while I'd faced starvation, monsters, and countless new and frightening situations in this world, what I did next was by far my bravest moment.

"Are you lying to me?"

"What?" Summer gasped, stepping back, waving her arms. "How can you ask that?!" The anger in her voice, the shock. The peacemaking side of me wanted to retreat, apologize, smooth everything over before there was no going back. And that's exactly what Summer was trying to do. I know that now, in hindsight. In fact, I think it's a pretty common tactic guilty people try. Accuse the accuser, make them question their question.

But I wouldn't. I couldn't. What kind of friendship is built on lies and secrets? How can someone really be your friend if they don't know who they're really being friends with?

So instead of taking back my question, I added a second.

"Why are you lying to me?" I didn't mean to sound angry, but the more I talked, the more anger I felt. "We had an agreement. I trusted you. Why did you lie?"

That pause. The moment of a thousand thoughts. I couldn't believe this was happening to me. I'd never imagined it was possible. I remember someone, maybe in a book I read once, said they could face death, but not the thing I was going through now. One word, new and horrible: Betrayal.

"Why, Summer?" Again, to her silent, tortured face. "Why did you lie to me?!"

"Because I don't want to go with you!" Her shout had me staggering backward. "I thought if you came with me, if you saw how much fun the Nether was . . . And aren't you, Guy?" Her voice softened, her pitch rose. "Aren't you having fun? We could keep having fun if we just stayed here. You could build yourself your own house, as big and wonderful as you like. I'd help you. My mountain and your castle. Hot showers and redstone lamps and I'd make sure you'd never have to see me eat meat around you ever again."

I'd never seen her like this before. Pleading. Desperate.

"Summer." Shaking, mouth dry. "I have to keep going."

"But we have everything we could possibly want right here!"

"Except the way home." Arms out, the point so obvious. "Why don't you want to go home?"

Summer's voice cracked, melting into teary sobs. "Because I don't know who I am back home! What if I'm a loser with no friends? What if I don't know anything and can't do anything? What if I'm just a sad, lonely nobody back there?" One square hand swept around the Ice Cube. "Here, I'm somebody! I'm smart and strong and totally in control! I'm queen under the mountain here! And you want me to give all that up?!"

And then it all made sense. All the little mysteries that had been nagging me since we'd met. That CLICK I'd first heard when climbing her mountain? She'd seen me, but she didn't want to be seen. She didn't want anyone to discover her and to have this exact argument we were having now. That's why she'd hid her windows with gravel and her front door with lava. That's why she'd let me move on before coming after me.

But she *had* come after me. Part of her wanted to be discovered. I knew that feeling well enough. The inner conflict. The back-and-forth of knowing what you have to do even though it's scary and new.

When you're trying to tell yourself something, listen!

"Summer"—my voice was calm, anger replaced by sympathy—"I get it. I know how you feel. I was king of my island, and part of me didn't want to leave. I went back and forth, a lot. I even made up projects to distract me, to procrastinate, just like us going after glowstone. But I learned that growth doesn't come from a comfort zone but from—"

"Oh, enough!" Summer waved her cubed fist at me. "Enough with your lessons and mantras and always trying to teach me something! I'm sick of it! And you know what, Guy, I'm getting bloody well sick of you!"

A punch in the gut, invisible, brutal.

"You don't mean that."

"I bloody well do."

She stepped back, turned away. "I've made my choice, Guy. Now you need to make yours."

To be alone again, my worst fear. But if I stayed, wouldn't I be giving up too much of me? All my hopes, my dreams, the whole reason for coming here in the first place. All gone, just so I'd have another person next to me every day. Being with her would mean giving up too much of me. It was simply too high a price to pay.

Fresson sixteen: Friendship shouldn't force you to give up you.

"Make your choice," Summer insisted, still not looking at me.

"I did," I sighed, and turned for the door.

"Fine." She didn't move. "Goodbye, Guy."

"Goodbye, Summer." I reached for the exit, but turned at the last minute. "You're wrong, you know, about being a nobody with no friends back home. You're always somebody, and you woulda always had at least *one* friend."

I stepped out the door before she could respond and ran all

the way back, fueled by the last seconds of liquid haste. Part of that decision was to outrun any lurking ghasts. But part of it was also to outrun my waning resolve. It's one thing to make a choice, another to accept the consequences. Alone again, back out into the cold, literally. Why do some right choices have to hurt so much?

I sped back to the portal, phased back to the mountain, and walked slowly and sadly to the front door. But as the lava receded, I realized it was night outside. In fact, as soon as I could see out into the cold dark wastes, a couple of skeletons saw me.

"Wrong number," I yelped as two arrows whistled past my face. Closing the door and flicking the lava switch back on, I could hear their bones burning on the other side.

Tomorrow, I thought, heading back for the guest room. *Better to start first thing tomorrow.*

The bed. Right there in front of me. If I'd just waited till we got home . . .

What? Then we'd have kept going with our little . . . what do they call it? "Charade." Back and forth, gathering glowstone we didn't need, which would only have given Summer more time to make up lies. It would have come out eventually. Sooner or later, I'd have been right here planning my exit.

I bedded down for the night, curling up with sadness, anger, and thoughts I tried not to think. *Maybe staying here an extra night'll give Summer enough time to come around. Yeah, that could happen. She could realize she was wrong, follow me back here, and wake me up to tell me that she's ready to come with me.*

But, on the other side.

Don't cling to false hope. She's gone. It's over.

Still, the next morning, I woke up expecting her to be there.

"Summer?" I called, heading back to the main chamber. "Summer? You here?" I checked her bedroom, the kitchen, the workshop. I even headed down to the chicken coop. Nothing. And the lack of new chicks told me that she hadn't been back to harvest another meal.

She probably came back last night and didn't wake me. That had to be it. She'd returned for her own rest and was still mad enough to ignore me.

Well, two can play at that game, I thought in a huff, tramping out of the mountain into the bright, freezing taiga. I didn't even bother to restock my inventory: food, arrows, potions, even extra crafting materials like wood and metal. I didn't want to take anything from her, and I certainly wasn't going to wait around to argue that our time together had earned me the right to take my share of supplies.

I can harvest what I need on my own. I don't need anything from her. I didn't even take any of the glowstone I'd helped her gather. She could keep them, for all I cared. A reminder of how she'd blown this once-in-a-square-world chance for friendship. And the netherrack? I still had some in my pack. That'd be enough of a souvenir. Their stink would always remind me of our faux friendship, a "friendship" based on betrayal.

I didn't stop to switch the lava back on. *If she still wants to hide from the world, then that's her problem.* It felt good to be mad. The anger was like an engine that kept my eyes forward and my legs moving. *If she's too stubborn to come after me, why should I waste another second waiting for her?*

That notion got me across the open snow, into the forest. But the moment I entered the trees, I could tell that something was different. First off, a whole new animal ran right past me. It was small and white, and had the basic outline of a wolf. I suspected it wasn't a wolf at all, but another member of the canine family.

"You're a fox," I said to the retreating, bushy tail. "Aren't ya?"

The animal didn't stop to answer, or even stop to look at me. It skittered over the nearest ridge with a high, huffing squeak.

"Just don't try to hurt me," I called after it, "or any of those sheep, and you and I will get along fantastically, Mr. Fox."

Strange I didn't notice them before, I thought, continuing through the tall, dark trees. *Maybe I just didn't spend enough time in these woods, or maybe their white coat blended in with the patches of snow. Or maybe . . .*

My next theory formed with what greeted me over the ridge. Bushes, clumps of them about a block high, with what looked like little crimson berries growing on them.

They certainly hadn't been there before. I would have seen them. This was the exact path I'd taken last time. And the reddish purple berries would have stood out sharply against the browns and greens of the forest.

Had it come with the last world change? That time when we'd discovered fish in the river? Probably. We hadn't done any exploring afterward.

And who knows what else is out there now, I thought, stepping up to the nearest bush. *And if this is a new source of foo—*

"Yow!" I jumped back, pricked by hidden thorns.

"Got it," I told the bush. "Proceed with caution." Which I did, gingerly reaching for the rouge prize. "And hopefully, thorns are your only defense."

I was thinking about poison, wondering if I'd soon be reliving my experience with raw chicken.

"With great risk, comes great rewards," I announced to the berry on its way to my mouth.

I wouldn't say the reward was "great," certainly not in terms of any superpowers, or even filling my belly. But the taste.

"Mm!" I popped down a few more sweet berries. "I can't wait to tell—"

I stopped at the thought of her name, the sweet discovery now tasting very bitter. I'd forgotten. Just for a moment.

I guess she'll discover these on her own, I thought, harvesting a few more berries before shuffling sadly over the next ridge.

Don't look back. Don't think twice. You've made your decision. Just keep going.

"Baaah."

"Hey, flock," I called, waving to the sheep I'd met earlier. "Good to see you're all okay."

"Bahhh," they called back, munching peacefully, ignorant of everything I'd just gone through.

I didn't want to feel the sadness that began creeping up from my heart. I didn't want to feel the loss. But seeing them together, remembering my own sheep back on the island. If only there'd been a potion that cured emotion.

"Well, at least you have each other," I sighed, and strode on toward the end of the wood. I could see the trees beginning to thin, the beginning of another white expanse. In a minute or so I'd be in uncharted land. More adventures. More opportunities.

"Moo!"

There they were. Three of them grazing among the last tall spruces.

Cows.

"Moo." It was the nearest one, ambling slowly toward me. She was probably looking for another savory patch of grass. But when she randomly looked up at me . . . when our eyes met . . .

Moo. My best friend back on the island. My first friend. Companion. Teacher. Foil. She'd always been there for me, even when she wasn't physically there. When I was trapped in the maze of mineshafts, just knowing that she was up there, somewhere, waiting with a bucket of milk and a reassuring snort. It didn't matter how far away she was. Our friendship had canceled the distance.

Friends keep you sane.

"Thanks, pal," I told the cow, feeling a sharp sting behind my nose. "Thanks for setting me straight."

Turning right around, I looked back toward the mountain. "I gotta give her another chance," I told the cows. "Friends shouldn't part in anger."

"Moo," they responded between munches.

"Exactly," I said. "Just because we say goodbye doesn't mean we have to say goodbye to friendship! I mean, I've learned all these fressons about friends respecting one another. Why can't I just respect her choice to stay? I'll go back, make up with her, and even help her finish lighting the mountain. Because I made a promise to her, and no matter what happens, friends keep their promises. And that's what we'll still be, even when I say goodbye. Parting as friends will mean that I can carry her friendship wherever I go, just like with Moo! Because friendship cancels distance, not the other way around! If we think about each other, and still care for one another, then we can still keep each other sane!"

"Moo," they applauded, and turned their black and white butts to me.

Heading back for the mountain, I might as well have had another haste potion. "Friends keep you sane!" I hollered. To the sheep, the igloo, the fish under the ice river. Even the bouncy, dopey bunnies who were probably terrified of me. "Friends keep you sane!"

There was the mountain, just as I'd left it, with the lava fall still off. Had Summer not noticed? Or maybe she kept it off on purpose, hoping I'd return to see it? A sign! An apology!

"Summer!" I called, bursting through the double doors. "Summer, it's okay! I don't want to end on a fight! I forgive you for what you said and I hope you forgive me too!"

I skipped down the hall and into the main chamber. "It's okay if you don't want to come with me! Friends respect each other's choices, right? Friends forgive, Summer! Summer?"

No answer. Again, I checked everywhere, calling her name, even double-checking rooms I'd been through just a few minutes earlier.

Nothing.

Silence. Emptiness.

"Must be back down in the Nether," I mused to the echoing walls. "She must have come up and gotten her rest when I was sleeping in the guest room, and left before I got up. Or maybe just now." By this point I was back in the main chamber, nodding at what I thought might be a reasonable explanation. "Maybe the change in this world allows you to sleep during the day. Maybe she came back just as I left, grabbed a power nap, and headed right back down."

It was a possibility, just like her sleeping the night before. Either way, I was sure she was fine and safe and would probably be back here any minute.

So why did I feel that something was very, very wrong?

CHAPTER 17

She'll be back, I thought cheerfully, setting up my bed right at the entrance to the portal room. She had to be back soon. She had to sleep. And if, for some reason, she hadn't come back the night before, she'd be totally loopy by now. She'd need to come back tonight.

But the next morning, when she didn't return, I started to worry. Yes, she might have still been angry, portaling back to the mountain, then creeping past me to her own bed. She might have even crept past me again, back to the portal, before I woke up.

Possible, but likely?

I didn't think so. That next morning, when I woke up to find the mountain still Summer-less, I knew something had to be wrong.

Again, running from room to room. Again, calling her name.

She was back in the Nether! She had to be! But why? Was she still angry with me? Was she trapped? Hurt?!

Nightmare scenarios floated before me, images of Summer trying to come after me, trying to apologize, but not realizing that there was a ghast behind her! What if she was . . .

I should have stopped, taken a breath, and really thought about what needed to be done.

And if I'd done that, this story might have ended up in a very different way.

But I didn't.

Panic drowns thought.

Back into the portal, through the purple swirl.

Back to the heat, stink, and near-night.

I gulped a night-vision potion, waited for the gloom to brighten, then looked frantically all about for my partner.

Lava, netherrack, and the occasional distant zombie pigman greeted me.

The Ice Cube! She must be there, resting, hopefully, or maybe nursing some wounds.

I ran across the narrow bridge, bounded across the nether-rack plain.

Heart pounding, panting in the heat, I followed the quartz path to the intersection, turned in the direction of the Ice Cube, and ran along the narrow cliff high above the lava.

What the . . .

Something caught my eye, slowing my step.

Something . . . some *things* . . . were out there in the molten sea. Little black dots, too far away for me to make out. Dots that definitely hadn't been there before. Dots that were definitely moving!

Creatures? Those magma cube monsters? Or was it something new? A change in the Nether just like in the world above?

I flashed to the foxes, the sweet berries. Those might not have come along with the river fish. They might have just appeared with another, brand-new change! And if that change came as recently as two nights ago, and if it also affected the Nether . . .

"Hrreehrr."

The snort turned me around, facing back the way I came.

A zombie pigman was coming toward me, one of the mini-types I'd learned to ignore.

But . . .

"Hrhrhreeehr!"

The sound, the sight. This one was different. No rotting skin, no exposed bones. This little pig boy or girl, or whatever it was, was alive!

"Oh, hi," I said on reflex, hoping that, maybe, life also brought language. "You haven't, by chance, seen a human kinda dressed like me but with long hair and a funny accent?"

The piglet—piglite?—stared up at me, snorted again, then punched me, hard, in a place that . . . well . . . that if I'd been back on my world, would have been really, really painful.

"Ay!" I yelped, more out of annoyance than actual pain, then raised my sword. If this little brat was anything like the mini-zombies up top, I'd be in for a serious fight. The small piglite came at me again, and this time met a sharp, diamond greeting.

"Krhreee," it squealed, and then, surprisingly, fled like a bat out of the Nether.

"Yeah!" *That's right*, I nodded after it. "You better run! You little—"

"Krhrorrrr." That was from its dad, who was bigger, and armed with a golden sword.

"Now hold on," I said with weapons ready. "I don't want any trouble."

It did. The shining yellow blade raised to strike. I blocked it with my shield, gave back a quick slash, then easily warded off another blow.

"Not so tough," I said, knocking it backward with a second swipe. "And you burn!"

As the adult piggite stumbled onto a flaming square of netherrack, the flames leapt up its golden armor.

"Bringin' home the bacon," I said with a final chop.

I wouldn't have eaten any bacon, of course, but I did now have the firm conviction that this broiling underworld had, indeed, changed. And not for the better.

Summer!

Down the trail, legs and mind racing.

She must have run into these piggites. Maybe they trapped her in the Ice Cube!

I expected to see a whole horde of them besieging her base. I was already planning how I'd fight my way past them.

Instead, as the Ice Cube came into view, I found myself more scared by the empty space. No mobs. No siege. Did that mean she wasn't home?

"Summer!" Throwing open the doors. Feeling the chilled air on my face. And seeing an even chillier sight before me.

Summer was gone, and from the looks of things, she'd even spent some time cleaning up. The walls had been repaired, the storage chests replaced. But where was she now?

A golden glint, across the room. Through the window. It was rising above the black fortress. A blaze . . . That spawner was supposed to be blocked up! How had it gotten around, or through, the barrier Summer and I had built? Stepping closer to the window, I could see more of them, floating like vultures above the sky-scraping maze. Summer had to be there. And now she was trapped by those blazes, and piggites, and every other devil, old and new, that this world could throw at her.

"Just hang on, Summer!" I yelled, racing back out into the heat. "I'm on my way!"

The double doors flew open, and I flew back out into the dry roasting air.

Waiting for me was one of those big, fat squishy magma cubes.

"Now?"

It leapt.

I swung.

And stood back as a whole family of smaller cubes landed before me.

"Not now!" I roared with one sweeping slice that sent them reeling and separating. "I promise I'll fight you later!"

I dodged around them and ran to the cliff stairs. Down to the beach, across the isthmus to the fortress, then up through the spiral tower stairs to the empty, nether brick hall.

"Summer!"

Running out onto the catwalk. Dodging the first volley of blaze flares.

Scared. Still running, reaching for my bow.

THF-THF-THF!

Past my ear. Drawing back for a shot.

The arrow whistled straight into its target.

"Ha!" I cawed, downing a healing brew.

And that's when my night vision conked out.

No problem, I thought, and reached for another potion.

There wasn't anything there! I hadn't brought any extra . . . of anything!

Back to the Ice Cube? Restock and return?

No. That would have been the smart choice. But all I could think of was Summer—alone, scared, hurt!

Panic drowns thought.

"Summer! Where are you? Summer?!"

I ran back into the hallway, into a total darkness I'd never experienced in the Nether before. It hadn't been so bad with night vision, but now I was nearly blind.

Torches! I reached into my backpack for wood and coal.

SHCLICK-SHCLICK.

Skeletons. Somewhere close.

I'd nearly stuck coal to stick when the first one clacked around the corner. I could barely see it. Those black bones. A wither skeleton!

Before I could reach for my sword or my shield, I felt it.

A cut from a stone sword that shouldn't have been more than a minor wound. But the feeling. The drain! Muscles, bones, organs. Like air stolen from lungs, it felt like my very life force was being pulled away. Aching, dazed. Instantly exhausted, as if I was suddenly one hundred years old.

This was what Summer had tried to warn me against. This was wither!

Staggering back, turning to run, I panted out onto the catwalk. Bow in hand, I drew for a shaky shot.

Missed!

A second arrow, just as the wither effects wore off.

THNK! Right in the skull. The impact punching my charcoal foe up onto the catwalk guard. A third shot, knocking it over the side. Dizzy, weak, I reached for another healing potion.

Out!

Just like with night vision. And this time, I didn't have the luxury of choosing to return to the Ice Cube.

Two more wither skeletons came clattering onto the catwalk, barring my way, forcing me to flee deeper into the fortress.

Chomping down on the last of my bread, I jogged onto the next tower, then down its open stairs into another nearly midnight chamber.

Take two for torches. But I didn't have any! I'd dropped all my sticks and coal during the attack! They were still back there, hovering, about to disappear! I could hear the clacking wither skeletons above and, through a grated window, the labored, metal breath of an angry blaze.

At least it couldn't get me, not in here. But the skeletons sounded closer every second. I had to block the entrance, but with what? My wood was gone, and I didn't have any cobblestone. And there wasn't time to hack out the nether bricks around me.

The netherrack! The blocks I'd kept as souvenirs! I threw them up at the ceiling just as the skeletons clacked overhead.

And in doing so, I realized I was solving two problems at once.

Netherrack burns forever!

Placing the first crinkly cube on the floor, I ignited it with a spark from my flint and steel.

"Light," I sighed, continuing to lay flaming netherrack down the hallway. "At least I can see where I'm going."

And if my flint and steel wears out, I can always gather more flint from the natural gravel.

I even spied a gravel deposit from the hall windows, down on the beach next to the isthmus. Iron was another matter. I only had seven bars left. *Not much good for anything else,* I thought, trying to stay positive, because, at this point, positivity was one of the few resources I had left.

At least I won't get lost, I thought, rounding another corner and placing another "rack-torch."

CLICK-CLICK.

Up ahead. Just around the next corner.

"Here we go again." I wasn't too worried. I had space to flee to, and even surplus netherrack to block up the hall.

And when a traditional skeleton came clickety-clacking into view, I actually let out a big "Thank you!"

THUNK! An arrow against my shield that sounded like "You're welcome" to my ears.

"Time to return the favor," I said, and reached for my own projectile weapon. But as I drew back the bowstring, no arrow appeared in my grip.

"Out again?!"

No wood, no coal, no potions, and now no arrows?!

"C'mon, fate!" I whined, and marched dejectedly toward the bone-built sniper.

Thunk! I deflected another harmless arrow as the skeleton wisely began to withdraw.

"Stand still," I demanded, slicing at empty air. "Will ya just let me kill you?"

For some reason, my fleshless foe didn't comply. Retreating, dodging, shooting, it led me farther and farther into darkness, down the hallway, past another intersection.

Always be aware of your surroundings.

But I didn't care. I was hot and tired and really annoyed that after I'd faced all these new threats, this run-of-the-mill twerp was wasting my valuable time. "Ya know how this is gonna end, right?"

I thought I did, but clearly this world had other plans.

Just as I managed to get close enough to land a strike, another sword jabbed me from behind.

Pain, drain.

Wither!

No time to eat, no time for looking back.

On instinct, I ran forward, away from the ambushing skeleton, past its silently laughing cousin.

I remembered to zig as the whoosh of its arrow struck the floor just in front of me.

I zagged to avoid another but took the hit where I should sit.

I winced, hissed, but kept going into the inky corridor. I could hear more clacking. More skeletons behind me. Three? Four? How many more arrows could I take? How many wither strikes?

I had to get away, find a safe space. Eat. Heal. I couldn't take any more damage!

Slowed step. Spinning head. Stinging shoulder.

Distance. Safety.

Blocked!

Another wither skeleton, this time right in front of me! Stepping into my path with stone sword raised to kill.

Did I still have the strength to fight? The speed to dodge? I gritted my teeth, raised my thousand-pound shield, and prayed, with all my might, for just one blessed shred of good luck.

But behind it, a diamond flash. An axe! Badly chipped but catching the faintest light. It smashed the wither skeleton to smoke as its ragged, huffing, utterly awesome owner stepped into view.

"Summer!"

"Guy? What in the world are you doing here?"

"Uh . . . rescuing you?"

CHAPTER 18

"Follow me!" Summer led me at a run, skeletons clacking in our ears.

Two turns later, we came to a wall of netherrack surrounding an actual wooden door.

"Through here," she motioned, and a half-second later I was standing in her temporary shelter. It must have originally been one of those staircase tower rooms, but the stairs had been taken away, and the rows of nether wart had been replaced by mushrooms growing on bare nether bricks.

The whole scene—Summer and her room—reminded me of that experience under my island. Trapped, lost, starving, and wounded, I'd dug deep, both into the earth and my soul, to carve out enough space and time to recover. That had to be the case with my battered, tattered partner. Still, I had to ask . . .

"What happened?"

"Have you met our new neighbors?" she asked.

"The piggites?"

"I call them swinelings. Three of them just appeared behind me, two with swords and one with a crossbow."

"What's a crossbow?" I asked.

"Like a bow, but, on its side and . . . I'll explain later. What matters is that I wasn't ready."

She sighed.

"I was injured, about to nick off home to the Ice Cube, when . . ."

She shook her head.

"One of those ghastly ghasts blew a hole in our blaze pen."

"I saw that."

"And they came whirling out, and with the whole ruddy army after me . . . well . . ."

She sighed again.

"The truth is, I wasn't thinking." Her voice lowered, hesitating with what had to be some very hard words. "I wasn't thinking because I was cross. Cross at you. Cross at . . . me . . . for driving you off."

I looked down at her unarmored feet. "You didn't drive me away. I wasn't in the best of moods either. In fact"—my eyes rose up to meet hers—"I came back because I didn't want to part in anger. And I wanted to say—"

"No," she interrupted. "Let me say it first. I'm sorry."

"Me too."

Fresson nineteen: Friends can fight, and they can also make up.

It felt so good to be back on good terms with Summer. Like I was on top of the world, instead of stuck underneath it.

"So," I chirped happily, "now that we're cool metaphorically, let's get up to a place where we can be cool literally."

"Well said," she chirped back, "if slightly overcomplex."

At that, we laughed, together.

"And as you'd say"—I reached into my pack—"let's get you 'kitted out.'"

Spotting her crafting table, I used four of my seven remaining iron ingots to craft her a new pair of armored boots. "Sorry I don't have enough for a helmet."

"I'll take what I can get," she said while harvesting her mushrooms. "And you're welcome to my little fungi crop."

"I'm good," I said, grateful to still have a few carrots left. "Water?" I held out the last bottle.

She shook her head. "Better save it for when we're really thirsty."

"Define 'really'?" I could have drunk a lake.

She laughed again. "Ready for a pleasant stroll back to the Ice Cube?"

"What about this way?" I turned for the back wall. "I'm just thinking, we could dig up through the netherrack to the landmass on the other side. That's where this tower connects to, right? We could come out the other side, then circle back the long way to the Ice Cube. It might take a little longer, but we won't have to fight our way across the fortress again."

"It might work." Summer hesitated, about to speak, but, as I'd recognize later, trying not to just shoot down my idea. "The only sticking point is that I don't know if the two landmasses connect anywhere but here. We might end up having to come back this way anyway, and with less resources than we have now."

"Good point," I conceded. "At least we know what's waiting for us this way." I stepped up to the door.

"Ready, steady, follow me!"

Which I did . . . up to a point.

I followed her down one muddy red hall to the next, past a reaching wither skeleton—which she yelled at me to ignore— and finally to yet another one of those brain-teasing intersections.

"Which way?" I asked, listening for the clack of bony feet.

"This way!" she declared, pointing to the right. "I think."

" 'Think'?" *If only I could raise my eyebrows.*

"Well . . ." She yawned. "I haven't slept in days and . . . I'm pretty sure . . ."

Doubt. Me of her and her of herself.

"No." She pivoted ninety degrees. "This way, straight forward."

"You're sure?"

"No."

"Good enough."

Twisting, turning, looking ahead and behind.

"Dead end!" I shouted at the netherrack wall as Summer said something rude I will not copy in these pages!

"Back the way we came." She turned, but as I looked out the barred window, I saw the glint of something instantly familiar.

Across the expanse, flickering through the window of another raised hallway . . . one of my netherrack torches! "Look!" I cried, pointing through the grate. "I placed those!"

Summer froze, not in fear, but, I guessed, trying to calculate what it would take to cross over. "Right," she said, turning back down our aborted path. "Off we go!"

We found the firelit path with no problem after Summer puzzled out the correct series of turns, and as we found our way up to the catwalk, I felt hope bubbling in my chest. "We made—" I didn't get a chance to say "it."

What is it with me and tempting fate?

FTH-FTH-FTH!

"On your right," shouted Summer. A tri-shot between the two of us, its spinning gold owner aiming for a second try.

Oh, for just one arrow!

Summer swore again, at what I first figured was the blaze, until I followed her eyes down the catwalk.

Three skeletons, one normal and two wither, were clacking out of the tower entrance ahead.

We couldn't go forward, obviously, and hesitating only allowed the blaze time to power up for another burst.

"Let's beat it," I suggested, already retreading our path in my mind to figure out an alternative route. "If we circle back to that far tower over . . . Summer!"

I should have known what was going to happen, that she'd just charge ahead, waving her axe, going for the first wither skeleton. I didn't see what happened next. I was now running forward myself, heading for the skeleton archer.

Its bow was up, an arrow pointing at Summer. I jumped in

front of her, blocking the shot with my shield, then slashed the archer to smoke before turning to face the second wither skeleton.

It swung for my face. I recoiled out of reach. A second swipe. I jumped aside, then forward.

A hit!

I felt bone crack from my blow. The wither skeleton flew back several paces, balancing on the edge. I sprang forward, swinging for its chest.

Another hit!

As the death bringer disappeared over the side, I let out a deep, exultant "Yeah!"

But that "Yeah!" quickly became a pain-filled "Yeow!" as three fireballs ignited the nether bricks under my feet.

Skipping out of the flames, looking frantically for my partner, I felt my innards clench. There she was . . . on the edge! She was alone, no wither skeleton to be seen. She must have won the fight, but taken a wither wound in the process.

I could even see it! Little gray bubbles rising from her swaying body. Did she know where she was, how close to falling?

"Summer, look out!" Running up to her, cursing inwardly that this rotten, cruel, utterly unfair world wouldn't let me do something as simple as grab her hand.

Gotta think fast!

I climbed up onto the guard. A mini-cube, maybe, away from Summer. The angle? A gamble.

I punched, and she fell back onto the flat, wide bricks.

"Whuuu . . ." she mumbled.

Fth-fth-fth!

Jumping off the edge, shepherding her inside the tower.

"I'm so sorry!" I panted. "I didn't know what else to do!"

"It's all right," she breathed through dissipating bubbles. "Thank you."

"Can you walk?" I asked, not sure how badly she'd been hurt.

"I can run," she blustered. Same old Summer.

"No need." I scanned the hall for enemies. "Save your energy."

I gave her all the food I had left: five carrots and twelve sweet berries.

"Where did you get these?" she asked before munching through them like a machine.

"Up in the forest," I said as my own stomach growled, "and you'll have all you can eat when we get out of here."

At least the last leg of our journey was peaceful. Turning down stuffy passages, all we saw was empty air.

Muscles unwinding, breath stabilizing. My mind began to drift to how good it would feel to get back to the surface, or even just to stop at the Ice Cube for a quick rest and refit.

Cool air. Potions of healing.

Descending down the spiral staircase, we heard nothing but the sound of our own feet.

Food! Baked potatoes, carrots, soft, ever-fresh bread.

Crunching onto the narrow isthmus, all I could think about was the waiting snowy sanctuary.

I wonder if Summer's stocked any of those delicious chocolate chip coo—

"Brrreeee!"

We didn't notice it until the ghast's missile was nearly on us.

"Guy!"

Summer was ahead of me, turning, shoving me back. Out of my daydreams. Out of the blast zone.

The explosion sent her crashing into me.

Coughing, blinking. My eyes cleared to see that the land bridge was gone, the hole now filling up with lava.

There was no time to even think about repairing the damage. No chance of leaping that taunting five-block length.

"Brrreee!" Another missile. Another retreat, as the second explosion blew more of the land bridge away.

"Into the tower!" I shouted, heading for the safety of the stairs.

"Brrreee!" The third impact threw us inside.

Climbing.

Huffing.

Swearing from Summer, which seemed to cool her temper. "Looks like we'll have to try your 'scenic route.'"

Walking back up into the fort, we headed for the catwalk.

"I don't see our gasbag," Summer observed with a quick glance into the open, "or any blazes for that matter."

"They're probably all hovering for an ambush," I sneered.

And I was right, at least about the blazes.

No sooner had we gotten midway across the catwalk, too far to turn back safely, than one of the revolving flamethrowers floated up from beneath to settle right in front of us.

"Here we go." Summer charged. I followed.

In this case, her reckless courage paid off.

FTH-FTH-FTH! Over our heads, shooting where we were instead of where we were going to be.

"Go on!" Axe high, Summer jumped toward the mob. "Clear

off!" A flurry of metallic, clinking swipes left a puff of smoke and a blaze rod falling into her pack.

Any chance to celebrate, or even congratulate her, was cut short by the clacking of wither skeletons behind us. At least there wasn't an archer with them. We could outrun swords.

And outrun them we did!

It didn't matter that we were burning up the remaining food in our bodies. It didn't matter that more monsters could be waiting behind every turn. We couldn't afford another fight. We had to get back to her shelter.

"Grmfth!" It was a piggite, clad in hides and wielding a golden axe.

It swung. I tried to block.

"Mf!" My shield missed the blade, allowing my chest to take the full blow.

"Ignore it!" cried Summer. *Easy for her to say.* "Don't dawdle!"

"You're lucky she stopped me!" I hollered over my shoulder, hoping my sharp words would hurt its feelings. Unfortunately, the consistent grunts told me that the brute wasn't deterred by verbal barbs. It was coming after us. Running!

We made it to the bunker, slammed the door, and tore into the back wall. My worn diamond pickaxe chewed through netherrack like a shovel through sand. Up, up, up, a steady staircase to the land beyond.

I wasn't sure how far we had to go, how much longer my one digging tool would last. I thought I heard a noise behind us, the distant creak of the bunker door opening, and then the last cube I picked gave way to a roiling rainbow.

"LAVA!"

We turned to run. To head back down the staircase. But, at the bottom, the piggite's axe-wielding form blocked our way.

"They can open doors?" I asked, stunned by the worst possible discovery at the worst possible time.

"To the side!" shouted Summer, as lava and pork closed in on us from both directions. "Burrow to the side!"

I turned to the right wall and picked for all I was worth.

I will say this about our crazy, blocky world: Its rules may not always be helpful in the moment, but in this case, making lava as slow as syrup was the only thing that saved our lives.

We were barely two blocks in before I felt the heat on my back. And Summer, one block behind me, must have been in true torment.

But she didn't complain, and as the sound of a distant squeal filled our ears, she even managed an understated, "Well, he's done for."

I might have chuckled in reply if at that moment my pickaxe hadn't decided to break. "Thanks," I muttered, mentally prepping for what I'd have to do.

Okay, so maybe digging through netherrack with your bare hands doesn't cause any permanent damage, and maybe it actually works pretty well. However, and I cannot stress this strongly enough: It. Is. Not. Fun!

Unless you like scraping your fingertips across sandpaper. Over and over again, block by block, minute after irritating minute.

"Fancy a hand?" asked Summer, about a dozen blocks into my ordeal.

"Oh no," I said, trying to sound brave, "I could do this all day." Then I descended into a poem of rude words and syllables that kept my partner giggling.

"Made it!" I groaned, stepping out onto the desolate, foreboding netherscape.

"This far," added Summer, as we took in the reality of our situation.

We were standing on the cliff of the opposite land mass. Between us lay the fortress, the lava lake . . . and the rising ghast!

"Onward then!" chirped Summer, heading inland.

"Wait for me!" I called.

And, not wanting to be left out, the ghast added a missile-launching "Brrreeee!"

"We gotta keep the ocean on our right!" I huffed, running up next to Summer.

"If we can," she answered to the trill of an incoming bomb.

It was hard to see where we were going without night-vision potions to aid us in getting the lay of the land. Spotting what I thought might be a ditch, I shouted "Cover up ahead!" and changed course.

We jumped into the shallow trench just as another cannonball streaked above. "Keep running," I called, realizing I might have led us into catastrophe. At least open ground gave us room to maneuver. In the trench we'd be pinned if that living air raid decided to pass overhead.

But the next "Breh" we heard sounded fainter, and the "Wehwehwoowoo" after that was almost inaudible.

Summer must have been thinking the same thing, because she began to slow. I almost said something fate-tempting like "I think we're safe," but instead opted for a series of parched coughs. Summer came to a complete stop, held out a hand for me to do the same, then slowly rotated her ears to the sky.

Neither of us heard anything. Summer stepped a few blocks up to look.

I stayed put, ready to bolt at a moment's notice.

Summer poked her head slowly up, eyes skimming the land and sky. She was about halfway through her 180 when her head just stopped, suddenly.

"Blimey."

CHAPTER 19

If my square eyes could have widened, you bet they would have at that moment. Climbing up next to Summer, I gawked at what had to be a hallucination from sleep deprivation, or maybe a trick of the half-light. But I could have sworn we were staring at an entirely new environment.

Large pillars rising into crimson canopies, some of which held hanging, vinelike ropes or glowing cubes that were definitely not glowstone. And the air around it glowed, too—or rather, something *in* the air. Fireflies?

My first thought was *Forest*, but it couldn't be. Could it?

"What are we seeing?" I asked both Summer and myself. "What is that?"

"Breh" came a familiar cry from behind us.

"We'll know soon enough!" Summer took off at a run, and I joined her. Hurrying across the final expanse of open ground, we soon found ourselves in and among the trees. And grass! At least, it looked similar to grass. Crimson color aside, the little clumps grew in the same patterns as their verdant cousins up above.

There were even mushrooms! Not the brown or red-white varieties, and close to—but not quite—nether wart. These were tall as my shin, with grayish rusty stems and reddish caps that lightened at the top. And oh, the smell! As I picked one up, the sharp, rotten cheese aroma practically socked me in the sinuses.

"I wouldn't try to eat those," warned Summer, "not till we have some milk or healing potions on hand."

"You've never seen this?" I asked. "Any of this?"

"Not till now," she answered thoughtfully, "and if I was going to venture a guess, it would be that this whole biome just popped into existence along with the swinelings."

"I'm inclined to agree with you," I answered, packing the stink-shroom away, "but the bigger question is, does this red forest or swamp or whatever you want to call it connect back to where we need to go?"

"Only one way to . . . find out," declared my fearless partner, coughing on the last two words. What I'd thought might be fireflies actually turned out to be burning cinders. More evidence that these topped poles around us were alive.

But what were those luminous cubes embedded in them? Glowfruit? I was about to reach up for one when the sound of a snort turned both our heads.

"Did you . . ." I started.

"Heard it," she finished.

At first we thought it was a piggite, and we readied our weapons for battle. We couldn't see anything, the vined columns and uneven terrain cutting visibility nearly down to zero.

"Hrrh" came another snort, closer this time and, frustratingly, from all directions.

"Up there!" I saw Summer looking up the incline. Beyond the vines, something was moving. Four legs. An animal, and about half the size of a sheep.

"A pig?" I asked.

Summer nodded. "Or maybe a wild boar?" And as it descended the slope, I saw why she might be right. Small white tusks protruded from either side of its stubby, angular snout.

Wondering how much damage those tusks might do, I retreated a few steps and started looking for the quickest escape route.

"Don't be so skittish," chuckled Summer as the boar trotted up to her. "This little chap doesn't look—"

"Hrrhhuh!" it snorted, as the tusks bashed her in the knee.

"Oi!" she roared, axe swinging.

The boar flashed red, gave a high, pained "Hrrah!" then bounded back up the slope.

"Well, we saw him off easily enough," Summer chuckled, "although it would have been nice to see how he might taste."

I didn't share her levity. Something about the creature gave me an uneasy feeling. The size, the reaction. It reminded me too much of the baby piglite I'd first seen down here, and how if there were small ones . . .

"I think we better get out of here," I said, turning too late to Summer.

I saw the mama boar just as it hit her from behind. She flew, catapulted by the tusks, toward the lava!

Pivoting to me, the cow-sized, fur-backed tank of an animal gave an angry snort, as if to say, "You're next."

There wasn't time to turn to see if Summer was okay. I raised my shield, lashed out with my sword, and, in anticipation of the coming attack, turned my back to the land.

"Hrraarrrhh!" Mama-boar snorted, and charged at me like a runaway minecart. And it sure felt like I was hit by one. Even with my raised shield and swinging sword, she managed to toss me right up onto the hillside above her . . .

. . . and right into my "trap," so to speak.

Wisdom under pressure.

I figured the only way to counteract her raw power was to fight from higher ground. And I also figured that the only way to reach that higher ground in time was to let her give me a "boost."

It hurt, no mistake about that. But it was well worth the wound for this advantage.

"C'mon!" I taunted. "C'mon and get me!"

She snorted, shook her battering ram head, and barreled up into my waiting sword.

"This little piggy went to MARKET!" I snarled, slicing and waiting for her to fall.

Only she didn't. I'd been wrong about that part. But when she'd struck, the blow only lifted me one block higher.

"And this little piggy stayed HOME!"

You can guess how the rest of it went. A battle royale between tusk and blade. Of all the creatures I'd faced in melee battles, nothing had been as tough as this little piggy. I'd never seen anything take this much punishment and dole out much more than her share. The tears in my armor, in my flesh. On the third blow I felt my ribs crack. I coughed hard and finished my battle chant. "And this little piggy cried weeweewee!"

The third "wee" did it. The porcine juggernaut squealed into smoke, hovering hide, and . . .

"Pork!" called Summer, pulling my eyes up to a tree. "Small price to pay for being hit by a speeding lorry."

"Summer!" I cried, then wheezed in pain for a moment. "You're okay!"

"I wouldn't go that far," she said, gesturing to her pillared prison. "I broke my axe trying to chop my way down, and I fear my poor old bones won't take the slightest bounce."

"It's okay!" I called, reaching for my own battered axe. "Don't sweat it. I'll get you down."

"Perhaps you can think up another nursery rhyme battle chant while you do it," she taunted. "That was quite an entertaining show from up here."

"Keep it up," I said between chops, "and I'll keep you up there."

Chopping through the tree's purplish wood, I managed to slowly lower the trunk for Summer to get safely grounded. She was in pretty bad shape, stepping down the last block with an audible groan. "Ain't we a . . . pair," I coughed, wincing at the pain in my ribs.

"Ready to eat meat now?" she asked, reaching for what I guessed were the slabs of boar.

"Maybe," I nodded, inhaling sharply at the pain I felt, "but not until we've cooked it. Last thing we need is food poisoning."

"Can't argue with that." She looked around and said, "But since we don't have any cobblestone for a furnace, we may just have to give it a go and hope for the best."

"It may not come to that," I said, examining the purple logs in my hand. "We've got wood now, which means basic tools, which means maybe" — I'd noticed that some of the land around us looked like earth — "these grasses produce seeds." I started punching up the crimson clumps, my mind racing with ideas.

"You really think we have time for farming?" challenged Summer, no doubt wishing this world would let her put her hands on her hips.

"Maybe not," I said, after the tenth clump produced no seeds, "but . . ." I saw another mushroom growing nearby. This one was green rather than rusty, with a red-speckled cap. I picked it up, raised it to my nose, and gagged.

To be polite, it didn't exactly smell like the sulfurous nether-rack, but it was definitely in the same family. Kinda like what we get from cows, and I'm pretty sure I know this because I'm pretty sure I remember smelling it on people's lawns.

Figures.

I can't remember who I am or where I'm from or any other important fact about my old world. But I can tell you what folks in that world use for fertilizer.

"Whiffy?" asked Summer.

"Whiffy," I responded. "But possibly useful, if the two mush-room theory works down here. We got wood for bowls now. And if we gather enough for a stew—"

Another boarlike snort sounded nearby, closing in.

"Which will have to wait," said Summer, looking over my shoulder. I turned just in time to see a whole herd—yes, herd—of those mammoth killer boars, three adults and two boarlets, bounding down the slope toward us.

"This way!" I shouted, sprinting through a curtain of crimson vines. "Stay along the coast!"

They didn't let up, those snorting, cavorting beasts. They stayed right on our tail, so close I imagined I could feel their hot, wet breath on my back.

"Just super," huffed Summer sarcastically. "The speed of spiders and the patience of zombies."

"We'll lose 'em!" I panted, with all the faked positivity I could muster. "You'll see."

I was wrong, of course. They didn't lose interest in us. But we did manage to gain some distance, which, thankfully, bought us time at the next obstacle.

We were running among the trees, trying to keep the lava on our right, when suddenly the ground came up right in front of us, forming a solid cliff.

Think fast!

"Gotta dig!" I tossed Summer my sword and tore into the netherrack with bare hands.

We were three blocks in and two blocks high when the first little boar brat showed up.

"Go on," Summer shouted with flailing sword, "sling your hook!"

I didn't see any of this. I was too busy scratching our way to safety. I heard the impact of the blade, the squeal of the retreating tusker, then the deeper, angrier snort of its parent.

"Hang on," mused Summer, as I finished tearing out two more blocks, "I think they're too big to squeeze through."

I turned to see the garbage-can-sized head sniffing just outside our tunnel. "I think you're right," I said, then turned back to work. "They can't get in but we can't get out."

Back to burrowing like a mole, if the mole in question could feel the sting of every scrape.

Please don't be lava, I prayed to the netherrack wall before me. *Please don't be lava.*

It wasn't, but at one point I opened up the lower block right above a sizzling magma block. "Ee-ow!" I yipped, bouncing back into Summer.

"Maybe now's the time for those crude tools," she suggested. "Don't you still have three iron ingots?"

"I do," I sighed, hollowing out a space for a crafting table, "but I don't want to use up the only metal we've got."

The wooden pickaxe worked great, or, at least, spared my poor raw fingers more torment. I tunneled around the crafting table, then over the magma blocks and forward into sweltering darkness.

For a minute or so, everything went smoothly: netherrack falling before us and biting boars echoing behind us. Until, that is, we hit a deposit of black stone.

"Obsidian?" asked Summer, to my back.

I shook my head. "Not as dark," I observed, "and it gives way easier to my pick, but not enough to come free right away. It must have come with the change. And"—suddenly my heart beat faster—"if it's anything like the regular gray stone, we can upgrade our tools, make new weapons, and craft—"

"When we have time!" Summer reminded, with the snorts of our jailers for backup. "For now, please just go around."

I couldn't disagree, and picked a sideways detour. But the discovery alone was enough to lift my spirits, and as the next netherrack cube fell away, I practically jumped for joy.

"Gold!"

"Seriously?" Summer tried to see in the narrow space. "Here?"

"Again, with the change!" I exclaimed, examining the glimmering, netherrack-embedded flakes. "We now have a source of metal!"

My mind started spinning on possibilities: tools, weapons, armor. But suddenly another pained "Hrrrarrrh!" pulled me back.

"The boars," said Summer, looking back down the tunnel. "Are they fighting each other?"

"Or something else?" I wondered. We should have kept going, and maybe if we'd been better fed and rested, we wouldn't have let curiosity get the better of us.

"They could be fighting amongst themselves," I thought, out loud, as we stepped cautiously back down our escape tunnel. "You know, like when skeletons have those arrow duels."

"Or"—Summer picked up the pace, excitement rising with each word—"someone is killing them to save us!"

"Another castaway!" I blurted out, practically bumping into her. "Another human!"

Turning at the black stone deposit, we could now see down the length of the burrow.

"Someone might already be living down here," Summer continued, "in their own comfy, safe fortress!"

Close now. Almost at the edge. We still couldn't see anything, but the squeals and grunts rang loudly in our ears.

"Or someone just got here! Spawned here!" I swapped my wooden pickaxe for my worn iron axe. "They might be in trouble! We might have to save—"

Ourselves!

Because just as we were about to peek out to meet our "savior," the gold-helmeted head of a piggite poked in.

"Bad idea!" I shouted, turning to run as Summer muttered a weird, rooster-based profanity.

"Block them off!" I shouted over my shoulder, as the sounds of multiple piggites filled the hole.

"Can't!" shouted Summer. "You have all the netherrack!"

I grunted, repeated her bird expletive, and hurriedly switched from axe back to pickaxe.

Thank whatever higher power created this world that luck was finally on our side. It took only a few swipes before we broke on through to the other side.

This forest was similar to the first, at least in the shape and size of the trees. But their color, the color of everything around us, was bluish green: trees, ground, the ash floating in the air. After so many shades of red for so long, the stark contrast took a moment to get used to.

"Block it up!" shouted Summer as the piggite horde closed in. I threw down the first netherrack block, felt the hot, displaced air of a crossbow arrow whistling past my cheek, then fixed the second one in place.

"Right then," Summer sighed. "Now let's see if we can find our way to—"

"Hrrrurrrh!"

More snorts. Too loud and close.

"Up there!" I shouted, pointing at the hill behind us. Another boar herd.

"Oh, for heaven's sake!" Summer hissed, as we tore blindly through the woods. "Just a moment, will you?! Just a moment to breathe!"

I don't know who she was talking to. Herself? The fates? Or, similarly, the invisible creators of this world? In any case, whoever she was pleading with wasn't answering, as we squeezed through a couple of purple-veined trees and skidded to a stop within mere blocks of lava!

We were on a peninsula. A slim finger pointing out into the boiling sea!

"Hrrrurrh!" The boars, seconds behind us.

"Well, that's it then." Summer turned with raised sword. "Never thought I'd die in a last stand."

"And you won't!" I sprang forward with an idea in my head and netherrack in my hand. "We are NOT gonna die today!"

CHAPTER 20

"Build a bunker!" I shouted, slamming down the first block. "Here!" I didn't see her pick up the thrown netherrack stack. I'd already turned back to lay the first line. "Quick!"

I guess it was kinda overkill. A single wall probably would've been enough. But I wanted to be a hundred percent sure, and, judging from Summer's rushing to help, she agreed. As the boar battalion stampeded toward us, we laid down the first four-block-high wall across the length of the peninsula, then the sides, then the back. Then the roof! We didn't have too much netherrack left, but we didn't need it, as the double trees growing out of our "floor" covered most of the space. And their light-fruits allowed us to see.

"There!" I fixed the final netherrack roof block in place. "Done!" Turning back to Summer, I declared, "Now we do it my way. No more running. No more fighting. We need to take a moment, take a breath, and take the necessary steps to figure out what to do next."

"All right then," Summer surprisingly agreed, "we'll do it your way. Now what do we do?"

"Um . . ." I hadn't thought that far ahead. I thought Summer would've fought against my being in charge. "We . . . uh . . ."

"Practice that 'way' you're always talking about?" suggested Summer. "The 'Way of the Cube'?"

"Exactly!" I proclaimed, latching onto the lifeline she'd thrown to me. "The Way of the Cube! I was just about to say that! Plan! Prepare! Prioritize! Practice! Patience! Persevere!"

"So"—Summer continued, calmly knocking out a block of the landward-facing wall—"in order to have a plan, we should probably take the time to study these world changes."

"Again, about to say it," I said with a small laugh, and hollowed out another hole on the lava-facing side. "Priority one: Watch and learn."

And we watched. I'm not sure for how long. Between no sun and lack of sleep, it was nearly impossible to tell time. Especially when all I could "learn" from that bubbling molten soup was what I'd already known for too long: end of the line.

Patience.

The monotony was only broken when Summer announced, "Our friends have shown up." And from the grunts and clanking of gold armor, I didn't have to ask who those "friends" were.

"They're at it again," she narrated to the pained squeals of the nether boars. "And it doesn't look like they're hunting for food."

More squeals. More battle din.

"Must be for self-defense," she pondered. "Or perhaps they just enjoy killing for sport."

"Then that makes them real monsters," I said, "which makes me feel a whole lot better about fighting them."

"Morality aside"—Summer kept her eyes glued to the battle raging outside our bunker—"they did also leave us a feast of raw pork chops. Which reminds me . . ." And she reached for the two pink slabs in her pack.

"Hold on!" I warned, and got out my wooden pickaxe. "We still need to figure out a way to cook it."

"Where do you think you're going?" she asked, as I began tearing up our dirt floor.

"Remember that black stone we tunneled past?" I responded, stripping away the first layer of bricks. "There's got to be more, maybe even down here."

"Well, do be careful," my partner warned. "You don't know if our little outcropping is resting atop more lava."

"Don't worry," I said, making sure never to dig directly down. "I know what I'm doing."

And, for once, I did!

"Blackstone Central!" I cried, exposing a rich deposit. "Aw yeah!" I didn't even mind my pickaxe breaking with the next strike. A few quick chops against our central tree gave me enough wood for a crafting table and another, all-wooden pick-axe. And I didn't have to worry about the top of the tree falling in because of this wonderful world's different rules of gravity.

"So awesome," I hummed as block after block of black stone flew into my pack. "Enough for tools and a furnace and . . . oh . . ."

"Sorry?" asked Summer.

I didn't want to get excited; the disappointment would hurt too much if I was wrong. "Can I see that rod you got from the last blaze?"

She nodded and handed it over. "What on earth are you . . . oh!"

"You know where I'm goin'," I said, placing the rod on the crafting table along with three blocks of black stone. "And here we go!" First came the brewing stand, thunking onto the floor between us.

Next came the ingredients we'd been randomly collecting.

Nether wart from when she'd converted her hideout to a mushroom farm.

Magma cream from when I'd fought that first magma cube.

And last, but ridiculously, awesomely not least, the lone bottle of water.

"We did it!" I cried, brandishing the bottle of fire resistance. "We can walk out of here!"

"No," sighed Summer. "*We* can't."

Tire screech.

"You take it," said Summer. "Get yourself out of here. Get back up to the surface and collect all the armor and equipment—"

"No," I said, pushing the potion toward her. "You know your way back better than me. You should be the one to take it."

"But you're the one who deserves it." Summer's eyes fell, her voice softened. "I'm the one who got us into this, so I'm the one who should stay."

"We both got ourselves into this," I batted back, stepping right up into her face, "and we'll both get out together." Slipping the potion into my belt, I said, "I left you once, and I will never, EVER leave you alone again."

Fresson twenty: Friends don't leave friends behind.

Summer sniffed, finally meeting my eyes. Two words escaped her mouth, her voice cracking on the second.

"Thank you."

I held out my fist. She connected.

"C'mon," I said, going back to the crafting table. "We're on too much of a roll to stop now."

Persevere.

Eight black blocks later, we had our furnace. "Hungry?" I asked, as she slipped the raw boar slabs into the upper slot. "And now"—I held up a handful of purple bark logs—"here we . . ."

No ignition.

"Aw, c'mon."

Likewise, the furnace rejected the striped, blue-green planks. "C'mon!"

"Maybe we got our hopes too high," Summer muttered, and reached again for the uncooked meat.

"Or!" I held up my new, all-wooden pickaxe. "We just haven't explored every option."

By the glowfruit's faint orange light, the wood didn't look any different from surface types. But remembering one of my earlier experiments on the island, I placed the tool in the furnace's lower slot, and let out a resounding "Awww yeeeaaah!"

Fire!

"Just 'cause the rules don't make sense to us," I sang, doing my signature happy dance, "don't mean they don't make sense!"

Dividing logs into planks and then planks into sticks, we

stood back happily as the room filled with the aroma of grilling pork.

"You can't be picky now," Summer said, offering me a steaming chop.

"I'm not," I said, refusing the morsel, "but you clearly need the healing more than me."

"Thank you." Summer's voice rose an octave on "you," as if she was fighting back more emotion than she could handle. She must have won the battle because, clearing her throat, she retook her position on the land-side window and said, "Soon as those boar breakers leave, I promise I'll swipe you all those hovering chops."

"I'm just glad they don't eat them," I said, back at my lava-side post. "'Cause pigs being eaten by humanoid pigs is just creepy and weird. I mean, that'd be like us eating monkeys and apes. Do people do that? Back on our world? They wouldn't. Ya think?"

"I think *you* think you need to overthink everything." Summer laughed.

I joined her in a mutual crack-up, and was about to say something I'm sure only I would think was witty, when whatever was about to come out of my mouth evaporated into a surprised gasp.

"Whoa!"

"What?"

"C'mere!"

Summer knocked out another block next to me.

"What are you on about?"

Those dots on the lava, the ones I'd seen when I arrived right after the change. Here they were, up close! Walking—yes, walking—across the lava! Not magma cubes, but similar in shape and size. Two stubby legs supported a head slightly larger but similar in color to netherrack. Small, almost human eyes sat above a wide, thin, frowning mouth. Sparse whitish hairs, or maybe quills—almost like a porcupine's—flapped slowly from both sides of its head/body.

And on top of that head/body . . .

"What is that?" I pointed to a tan, seemingly painted-on object.

"Can't tell from this angle," she responded.

"Me neither." At lava level, it was hard to see. "Only one way to find out."

Standing under the canopy of our central, algae-colored tree, I chopped out enough wood to make enough sticks for four sections of a ladder. "Let's have a better look."

"I'll go," said Summer. "I'm stronger than you now, thanks to the chops, so if there's a ghast or blaze or one of those swineling sharpshooters, I can take the hit."

"Please be careful," I said, stepping away from the ladder. "And don't get too close to the edge!"

"Not planning on it." She shimmied up the wall.

What came out of her mouth is still a mystery to me. It sounded like "core," but what kind of expression is that?

"What is it?" I called up. "What do you see?"

"A saddle!" she called, sliding down next to me. "Guy, it's wearing a ruddy saddle!"

"Get out!" I ran to the window, peering with all my might. Yes! Now that I knew what to look for, it was definitely a saddle, which meant . . . "We can ride out of here!"

And turning to Summer, I saw that she was holding the other saddle she'd found in the fortress. "Yes, *we* can!"

"Brill!" I said, quoting her. "Now all we gotta do is prepare a snare!"

"Right!" Summer chirped. "If they're anything like the horses and pigs up top, all we need are fishing poles and carrots!"

"Well"—I happy-danced—"we got wood for sticks, and I always carry my spider silk . . . but . . ."

My dancing slowed. "We don't have any carrots."

Skidding to an emotional halt, Summer gave a long "hmmm" before saying, "Maybe we don't need any."

"How so?" I asked, hoping she had a good idea.

"Maybe"—Summer began pacing by the window—"if these lava-striding creatures were created specifically for this environment, they might also be attracted to a local food source."

"But we don't have any local food."

"Don't we?"

The question hung for a moment before . . .

"You're a genius!" I hopped up, reaching into my pack for the crimson stink-shroom.

The idea was right, if not the first result. After assembling our fishing poles, we discovered that they refused to take the ruby bait.

"Gordon Bennett," huffed Summer angrily.

"Who?"

"Never mind." She sighed wearily. "There must be an alternative, something else . . ."

"Right at our feet!" I reached down for a couple of the speckled-turquoise variety.

And this time they took!

"Come on then," said Summer, as I knocked down a corner of the lava-facing wall. "Come and get it."

But the saddled lava walker was too far away to notice. Instead, it sauntered frustratingly right past our bunker and down the coast.

"Looks like *we'll* have to go to *it*," I said, peering out the landward window for any threats. "No piggites, but I better make you a stone sword before we—"

"No time!" She practically jumped in front of the window. "It's getting away!"

Widening the opening into a doorway, I noticed that the hovering chops weren't the only loot left behind in the piggite-boar battle. The four-leggers had given as good as they'd gotten, killing enough of their hunters to leave a golden helmet, a golden sword, and one of those sideways crossbow thingies.

"Here!" I said, tossing my bareheaded partner the headgear. "I'll collect the loot while you lure the walker."

"Righto," chimed Summer, going after the saddled beast.

I snatched up the chops, the sword, and was just reaching for the bow when I heard the first piggite snort.

"Guy!" I spun, diamond sword ready.

Summer was down the beach, unarmed and surrounded!

"Don't come any closer!" She was talking to me, warning me away.

"They're not attacking you!" I called, shocked at how she was moving easily among them.

"How astute," she said with a hint of annoyance, "which is why I told you not to get any closer."

"But why . . ."

"I think it's the gold helmet."

"Really?"

"There's nothing else different about me, is there?"

"Or," I said as I took a half-step closer to her, "it's the mushroom on the end of the rods we both—"

They all turned, snorted, and charged.

"Or not!" I ran for the bunker.

"Block yourself up!" Summer hollered. "I'm fine out here!"

"Good to know!" I yelled in response, rushing into the bunker, trying to quickly turn the doorway back into a window. I took a punch from one of the little piglites that crawled through after me.

"Aw, dude!" I winced, a sword swipe sending it scrambling back.

"You all right in there?"

"Yes, if by 'all right,'" I fumed, "you mean that I can't get out, you can't get in, and our only means of escape is escaping."

"Oh, stop your blubbering," chuckled Summer, "and get up on the roof to toss me your pickaxe."

"Pickaxe?" I couldn't have been more confused. "What could you possibly—"

"The gold!" Summer could not have sounded more exasperated. "For another helmet!"

"You sure it's your gold helmet?"

"You have a better idea?"

My silence was my answer, and it sent me to the crafting table for a black stone pickaxe, just in case the all-wooden model wouldn't do.

"Here!" I called from the window, tossing the new tool out to Summer.

"Be back in a jiff," she chirped, scampering well past the piggites into the tunnel. And in a few short moments she was back and tossing a handful of nuggets through the window. "Hope it's enough."

It was!

Swapping my diamond helmet for the gold version, I gulped nervously and opened the window back into a doorway.

They were out there. The whole mob of piggite horrors. I looked at them, some looked at me . . . and none of them came forward to attack!

"Awesome!" I sighed, sauntering casually among them. "Hey, Bob, nice to see you. Fred, how's it going? Love the axe, Karen—is it new?" The piggites just stared at me with their beady pearl eyes, then slogged away into the woods.

"Oh, yeah, totally get it," I quipped after them. "Places to go, things to kill. But you got my number—let's grab lunch."

"Are you quite finished?" commented Summer after an audible clearing of her throat.

I was about to wrap up my fifteen-minute set when both of us turned at the sound of a rumbling "Hhrrurrhh."

Killer boars! Another herd that heard us! And from their angry avalanche down the hill, it didn't look like our helmets worked on them.

"Right then!" Summer yipped, and rushed back over to the shore. "Over here!" she called to the saddled walker. "Look what I've got for you!"

"Um . . . fine time to mention this," I muttered as the boars were halfway down the hill, "but we don't know if the bait actually works!"

"Yes we do!" cried Summer, as her prospective mount spun toward her. "Here!" she called. "Right here!"

And suddenly she was on, riding the creature like a horse!

"Get the other one!" she called, pointing to a second walker.

"I don't have the other saddle!" I realized, aloud, just as the boars hit level ground.

Summer uttered one of her weird foreign curses and tossed me the leather seat. I reached to pick it up just as the first boar tagged me right in my bottom.

"Guy!"

Flying through the air, arcing down right toward the lava!

I hit the beach with just one block to spare. Not burned alive, but so battered and gored that one more hit would finish me.

"Don't look behind you!" Summer called over the growing grunts. "Just get the beastie!"

I held out my rod to the unsaddled walker. It saw me, started over.

So slow!

C'mon!

"Guy!"

Close enough. Throwing on the saddle.

"Behind you!"

Closer snorts. Thundering hooves.

"Look out!"

CHAPTER 21

"Woooooo!"

Riding!

On lava!

I didn't care that my toes felt like french fries or that my lungs were crisping with each breath.

"Not today, Bacon Bits!" I called back to the beached pig-gites, seeing just how close they were to being able to hit me. "Not today!"

"Guy!" called Summer from across the red sea. "You're going the wrong way!"

"Oh right," I shouted, realizing I was heading back toward the shore of the crimson woods. "How do I turn around?!"

"Just turn the fishing pole!" shouted Summer. "Point it where you need to go!"

"Oh right!" I twisted the shroom-hooked rod back toward my partner. "Got it!"

Then, as I passed her, I realized I didn't know how to stop!

"Whoa," I ordered, then, louder, "Whoa!"

The big-headed beast just gurgled back at me.

"C'mon, Gurgle!" I pleaded, as if naming the animal would help. "Will ya just stop already!"

"Put the rod away!" Summer laughed.

"Putting!" As the fishing pole slipped into my belt, the mount beneath me halted.

"Not so hard." Summer and her steed trotted up next to me. "Just takes a little practice."

You know what else takes practice? Changing helmets atop a strange new animal in the middle of a lethal lake.

Coming to a complete stop made me realize what a number that last boar battle had done on me. It hurt to ride, to breathe, and I figured that I couldn't afford to pass up even the slightest extra bit of protection. So, I tried swapping out my golden helmet for the diamond version in my pack . . .

But I dropped it. The gold one. Right into the seething sop.

"No matter," comforted Summer, "I'm sure you can find more gold along the way." And pulling out our fishing poles, we started off at a brisk trot.

"I don't think we can reach the Ice Cube," said Summer, motioning with her head to the crimson forest. "I don't think the two lava lakes connect."

She was right. The lava we rode on was separated from the black fortress by a tall, sheer cliff. That had to have been the landmass we'd run across just before reaching the crimson woods, but running down the trench had blinded us to the lay of the land.

"I think if we keep to the coast on our right," continued Summer, "it must wind back around to the portal."

"Are you sure?" I asked dubiously.

"Not a bit," was all I got back.

"All right then. Nothing to do but sit back and enjoy the ride."

And ya know, we actually did.

I'm not saying this new Nether is my first choice for spring break or anything, but the changes were kinda fascinating to watch.

For starters, these lava walkers were the craziest creatures I'd ever seen. Not only could we ride them but, in a couple instances, I saw them actually riding each other. I even saw one swimming up a lava column, using it like an elevator on its way to . . . what, the cavern roof?

Lava is a funny thing down here. The piggites and battle boars stayed well away from it—clearly they both can burn—but one time, we saw a zombie pigman being carried down a slope on it. No flames, no sign of distress. It looked no different than if we were riding down a surface hill on a stream of cool, blue water.

Just because the rules don't make sense to me doesn't mean they don't make sense.

I'll also admit that the crimson forest didn't look so bad from a distance, and the turquoise variety was genuinely pretty. And they were both so big! Vertically as well as horizontally. It would have taken days, maybe weeks, to build enough ladders and staircases to reach each level. And I'm just talking about the attached levels!

There seemed to be more of those floating islands, some with crimson or turquoise trees on top. I would have continued to stare at them if another wild sight hadn't grabbed my gaze: a lava walker, gurgling past us, with a zombie pig guy riding on top! And farther out, past another grown walker riding atop its friend, was a smaller, baby walker riding its parent.

"Kinda gets you thinking," I said, pulling up next to Summer.

"About what?" she asked, eyes firmly fixed on our path.

"If there are baby walkers, then there might be a way to breed them."

"And eat them?"

"What?! No!"

Summer laughed. "Just winding you up."

"Ha ha," I flat-chuckled back. Then, to my mount, "Don't listen to her, Gurgle."

Summer shook her head at that, no doubt about to lob another snark grenade.

But just then we entered a new environment, so different and unexpected it practically made my square head spin around.

For one thing, the air changed, again. From the bluish green of the turquoise forest to a heavy, grayish mist. And the land looked like whoever created it was either very distracted or else had a real mean sense of humor. The land itself was made of some kind of wavy black and gray material. Jutting here and there in sharp, ragged, uneven patches. The whole biome looked like a monster mouth with broken teeth. And if there was any safe place to land, neither one of us could spot it.

"Curiouser and curiouser," mused Summer, prompting me to wonder where I'd first heard that phrase. Was it in that book about the little girl who fell down the rabbit hole, or where those two dudes go crazy in Las Vegas?

Either way, the phrase applied here, especially where the magma cubes were concerned.

So many of them!

Hopping across the small, horizontal islands or splashing across the burning liquid.

"Hmm," I mused, "there's a lot of harvestable magma cream."

"Which still requires more water for potions," sighed Summer.

"Right." I sighed back, my mind now filling with the fantasy of a cool drink.

"Above you!" cried Summer, twisting her walker away from me.

I looked up, too late, as a blinding blob fell on me from above.

I wasn't hurt too badly—thank you, diamond helmet!—but I could feel the animal beneath me shudder.

"You okay, Gurg?" I asked, looking up just in time.

Eyes. Large, emotionless, sunset-colored eyes stared down on us as the living block leapt again.

"Get out of there, Guy!"

Raising my fishing pole to the side, I coaxed Gurgle out of harm's way. "You may be faster on lava," I said to the pursuing hopper, "but you're still slower than me!"

"For heaven's sakes!" Summer shouted. "Don't waste time taunting it!"

I looked up and around to see more cubes advancing from all directions. Another few moments and we'd be surrounded.

"This way!" called Summer, galloping through the largest gap. I tried to follow her, but the gap was closing fast. Two cubes, left and right, were closing in.

"Go, Gurgle!" I grunted to my mono-speed mount. "This is yer life too!"

Even if it could understand me, who knows if it could've gone any faster. The closer we got, the slimmer the gap became.

"C'mon, Guy!" Summer said, riding back toward me.

The magma and Summer leapt in unison, and I saw the glint of a golden sword!

Not enough to split, but the flashing red hopper was knocked out of my way.

"Thanks!" I breathed.

"Thank me later!" Summer galloped in front of me. "We're not clear yet!"

Maybe this world is a videogame, as Summer thinks, or maybe, as I believe, it's just set up to mimic one. Either way, the next few heart-pounding minutes could have been synched to an electronic score.

Lava cubes everywhere! Bouncing from the islands. Falling in front of us from the cliffs. Closing in on all sides.

Turning! Dodging!

Squeezing between two rock pillars.

Right! Left!

Over a collection of rocks. Gurgle slowing, hurting! It could move on land, but only in pain!

Back into the fire. Open space, around a lava fall . . .

Stop!

I practically cartoon-screeched to a halt as a magma cube plopped in front of us from out of the roiling column.

"We're almost out!" Summer, a little ahead of me, motioning with her rod.

There were no more pogo-cubes ahead, no more jagged rock spikes. We were back in the familiar, pre-change wasteland. To our left, nothing but open lava. And to our right, the same mundane, overhanging netherrack cliffs that rose up to—

"Look!" Summer's voice. Shocked. Happy!

I stopped, craned my head.

Above us on the cliff edge rested a torch-topped quartz cube!

"And there!" I shouted, pointing to several more. This was definitely the trail, close enough for us to follow.

"Come on then!" trumpeted Summer as we rode parallel to the path above. "I think I know where we are!"

I didn't answer. I was looking for a spot where we could travel by land. A beach, a slope, even a straight up-and-down cliff face for us to tunnel upward. The problem was that the trail was built on an overhang that hung way out into the sea. And that overhang's roof was too high for us to even think about reaching. Believe me, I tried to think of everything. I also tried not to think of what might happen if, heaven forbid, the trail turned inland away from us.

"We may have to tunnel up," I admitted after a few minutes,

"even if we end up far away from the path. Far enough under the overhang, where the netherrack meets the lava, we can at least burrow into—"

"No—there!" Summer came to a full stop, pointing ahead to a dim blue light.

It was hard to see through the mist, but, riding just a little farther, I thought I could make out several of those lights. Fires, but definitely greenish blue.

"More changed land," I observed, "and it looks like the only way up to the trail."

"Is it?" countered Summer. "Seems a bit riskier than finding a place to tunnel up through the cliff."

"Is it?" I lobbed back, motioning to the overhang I'd just talked about. "Even if you do find a place to tunnel up, which doesn't seem very likely, what about the risk of lava pockets above our heads?" On her silence, I pressed with, "At least this new land might connect right to the path, and if it's as wide open as it looks, we'll have plenty of warning if . . ."

"Brrreeee!"

We acted on instinct, jerking our mounts to either side.

"I can't see it!" I cried as the flaming cannonball streaked in between us. The angle was odd. Shallow.

"I can't either!" Summer's eyes were on the sky.

Nothing.

We scanned the mist for any hint of the floating bomber.

Nothing!

"Brrreeee!" Another attack, this time behind us.

And again, as we rode out of the way, I saw that the projectile was practically skimming the surface.

"Where . . ." I began, and then, tracing the missile's invisible trail, I realized we were looking in the wrong direction.

"Brrrreeeeh!" Rising from the sea, the pale forehead and black-lined eyes.

"Look down!" I called to Summer. "It's in the lava!"

"Never saw them do that," Summer muttered in her usual casual tone. "Looks like we'll have to make haste for shore."

"No time." I gulped as the flat mouth opened for another fireball. "I'll draw its fire!"

Old tactic. New environment.

As Summer rode in a wide arc behind the ghast, Gurgle and I galloped right for it.

"Sorry you have to do this," I whispered. "I know you don't really have a vote. But I promise, I wouldn't do this if I didn't have to!"

Gurgle just gave a gurgle, which I took for "Just shut up and focus!"

At first, we avoided the fireballs easily. But running out of distance also meant running out of dodge time.

"You know I can't keep this up!" Gurgle gurgled, or at least I imagine that's what was meant.

"I know!" I grunted as a fireball passed close enough to burn the hairs out of my nose. "Just a little bit closer, a little bit . . ."

Nearly there, nearly in sword range. But then something gold glinted behind the rising white submarine.

A flash, and then the dying ghast hissed as Summer rode up next to me.

"Pity," she murmured as the popping monster sank, "this way cancels out any chance of gathering tears."

"Oh good heavens, no!" I shot back, trying to mimic both her accent and sarcasm. "I suppose we'll just have to get home safe and alive and whatnot."

Summer tried, I guess, to give me a playful swat, but I rode just beyond her four-block hyper-reach. "Oh, get back here!" she laughed, as I zigzagged just out of her grasp.

"Run, rabbit!" I sang back, leading us toward those mysterious blue fires.

CHAPTER 22

This was another new land, and was easily the most inhospitable of anything we'd ever encountered.

Through aquamarine mist, we could see what looked like a valley, but a valley composed mainly of soul sand. That's where the lights were coming from. Patches of them were burning, eerie flickers that looked more suited to the burners of a stove. They even smelled a little like a stove, that whiff of gas before it lights. And maybe this might be a mistake of my hazy memory, but isn't that gas poisonous if breathed?

Death seemed to hang there, and yeah, I know it sounds a little overly dramatic, but you'll see soon enough what I mean.

We rode to the edge of the shore, and said, at least in my case, an emotional farewell to our underworld steeds.

"Right, off you go then." That was all Summer said to hers,

riding the walker onto land, then hopping off and shoving the quivering, clearly suffering animal back into its liquid habitat.

My actions were similar, but as the burbling, quill-headed face turned back in my direction, I couldn't help but say, "Thank you."

I hadn't had long to get to know the animal, but in the short time we'd been together, I couldn't help but think back to Moo. I wondered how she was doing, along with the rest of the animal gang. And I know this is just silly and sentimental, but as the walker strolled away into the heat, I whispered, "If you ever find yourself up top and need a friend, I got a whole island of them that I know would be glad to meet you."

"Here we go then," chirped my partner. "And from the looks of things we're in for quite a slog."

What she meant was the soul sand—the whole slowing beach of it. CRUNCH, CRUNCH, CRUNCH, one plodding footstep at a time. And it didn't help that I could feel the stuff scrape down into my boots.

"Don't worry"—Summer must have known what I was thinking—"it'll vanish when we get out, like pop-drying when you get out of water."

"Well, that's reassuring," I grumbled, feeling the hard, scratchy grit between my toes.

"You'll live," scolded Summer.

"He didn't," I volleyed, motioning to the weird, white, four block arches we were passing. Not quartz, which you could see the closer we got. I reached out to punch one of the blocks and, just as I suspected, it turned out to be solid bone.

This was a skeleton, the leftover of some gigantic life-form. "Go figure," I huffed, "a brand-new place with ancient bones."

"And ruins," added Summer, pointing to another kind of skeleton. Yes, this time, I am being poetic. Because this was the skeleton of a fortress. Smashed, hollowed-out ruins that, back in its heyday, must have been a magnificent bastion.

Unlike the tall, slim towers that rose from lava, this land-based redoubt was comprised of two shorter, thicker keeps. Isn't that the word for castle buildings? "Keeps"? One of them looked reasonably intact, while the other appeared to be gutted down to its "bones."

"And no," said Summer, preempting what she knew was coming, "I definitely do *not* want to investigate."

"Why?" I argued. "The portal's not going anywhere. And with all the changes, who knows what's waiting for us up ahead. If this place"—I jerked my head to the black castle—"is anything like the lava forts, we might find chests of stuff we'll need."

"And if we find other baddies?" countered Summer.

"Then you can blame me for everything on our way to the afterlife?"

I was really impressed with that comeback. I think I even nodded at myself.

Summer just took a moment, sighed, and changed course for the ruins.

And, wow, were they ruined.

You could barely make out what the original structure used to be. What I thought was the intact keep seemed to be a patchwork of various materials. There was that wavy grayish rock, some black stone, bricks made from black stone, and, as we got close enough to be sure, black stone embedded with flecks of gold.

"There's got to be enough here to make me a new helmet," I said, admiring the tantalizing luster. "And then some."

"We can collect it on the way back," said Summer nervously. "Let's not dilly-dally now."

"Wouldn't want to 'dilly-dally,'" I replied, half-teasing, half-agreeing. "Is that a light?"

Around the corner, on the first of the connecting floors.

"Probably more lava," said Summer, as we crept around for a look. What we found was a lantern, instantly recognizable by the metal cage.

"You think these came with the change?" I asked, punching it off the ceiling. Just like a torch, it blinked out in my hand.

"Couldn't care less," said Summer. "I'm just grateful for the light."

"I concur," I said, reattaching it to the wall. "And there's another!"

Below us, down sloping black stone, we could see one illuminating a lower floor.

"Careful," warned Summer, looking and listening with each step.

This basement, or subbasement, level looked like nothing but a showroom of every way to die in the Nether. Patches of magma blocks, small pools of open lava, a few dark holes that dropped into who knows what, and, as we peered across the vast, wrecked space, the faint, distant movement of either a battle boar or a lone piggite.

"Let's get out of here," suggested Summer, turning back for the steps.

"Wait!" I pointed to something nearly hidden by a black stone brick column. A color that wasn't supposed to be here. Tan and bright.

"A chest!" I hopped down the last step, scampering across the hazard-laden ground. "Jack-POT!"

Gold! Not just flakes or nuggets or even bars, but pure blocks of it! Enough for weapons, tools, and whole suits of armor! And that wasn't the only metal. There were a few plates of this brown, battered, really tough-looking stuff. Something unique to this world, probably, something that sent my curiosity into overdrive.

"And what's this?"

It looked like obsidian, but veined with some luminescent purple material.

"We can figure it out later," snapped Summer as I continued to rummage like a kid in a toy store.

"Food!" I cried, handing her two cooked pork chops. "For both of us!" There were also nine golden carrots hanging out in the bottom of the chest. Sweet. Crunchy. And gilded with extra healing!

"Oh, that's better," I hummed as my regenerating body banished the aches and pains. I continued to look through the chest and found arrows—three for each of us.

And, finally, the greatest treasure in this or any other world. A book!

"It's all here!" I gasped, thumbing quickly through the pages. "Everything we need to know about the changes!"

"Can we know them later?" Summer was not amused.

And I wasn't listening.

"Get this! The crimson forests are actually called 'Crimson Forests.' Nailed it! The blue-green ones are called 'Warped,' for some reason. Our lava walkers are 'striders.'"

"Guy . . ." Her voice was lower now, more businesslike than annoyed.

"That jagged maze we just rode through is a 'basalt delta' . . ."

"Guy," slightly louder, more urgent.

"And this new metal here is called—"

"Hhrrurrhh!"

Book closed, eyes up.

A herd of battle boars, or to be accurate, hoglins—thanks, book—had just entered the opposite end of the basement. I saw them just as they saw us.

"Right!" I yipped as their meandering trot became a focused gallop. "Let's go!"

Back up the stairs, and right into . . .

Piglins. That's what the book called them, and judging by the way they came after my non-gold-helmeted self, they clearly called me "target."

"The other tower!" Summer shouted, stepping back to allow me to get past her. "I'll cover you!" I wouldn't have known what she meant if I hadn't glanced back just for a second. Ever heard the phrase "passive resistance"? I'm not sure where I read it, and I'm not sure exactly what it means. But in this case, it applied to Summer, just standing there in front of the piglins. She wasn't attacking them, just passively blocking their path.

The piglins, for their part, didn't seem to notice she was there, or else did and didn't see her as anything more than a stubborn member of their party. I heard them snort, probably saying, "Hey, buddy, out of the way." But none of them raised a weapon to attack.

"Thanks, Summer!" I called, running through a hole in the other keep's wall . . .

. . . and wishing, a second later, that I'd done anything else.

From the outside, this keep still looked reasonably solid. But as soon as I stepped into the main chamber, I saw that it was completely hollow. Most of the nine floors were gone, wrecked down to holed catwalks crisscrossing above me. And the ground floor, my floor, reminded me of a child's game I think I used to play. Ever hear of The Floor Is Lava?

This was almost the case.

A rocky patch remained in the center, a patch that held solid gold blocks and an unopened chest. And why didn't I rush over to grab the gold and open the chest?

Well, that had a lot to do with the spawner hanging from a catwalk above the island. A spawner that created magma cubes!

"Okay then," I said as the first bouncy blob sloshed down before me. "I'll just be leaving."

And as if I needed any more reason to do so, the arrow that landed between my feet showed me that these hollowed-out floors were still crawling with piglins and skeletons.

I didn't say something dumb like "How could this get any worse," but I might as well have. Soon as I turned back for the front door, I found the way blocked by the original approaching piglins. What had happened to Summer? Was she still trying to get in the way of the others? How many more were behind these?

MAX BROOKS

They can't all get me, I thought, mind racing, weapons raised. *Narrow hall, one at a time. I can take 'em!*

Turns out I didn't have to! At ten blocks away, something made them all turn and head in the other direction.

"Wait, where are you going?" I almost said, right before I saw Summer's arrow sticking out of one brute's back.

Handy tidbit regarding those golden helmets: Their disguise only works *until* you attack the piglins. I'm not sure if somehow they realize who you really are or if they just don't care. Point is, once you attack, the jig is up.

I rushed out of the bastion to see my battle buddy already making a run for it. She had a decent head start on the pursuing pork. That was the good news. The bad news was that the slowing soul sand allowed them to devour the distance!

Yes, once they got stuck in it as well, they were as snail-paced as her. But from where I was standing, I could see that little bit of open space between them closing.

What to do? How to help?

A plan was forming—not fully formed, mind you—as I reached for the crossbow in my belt. Unlike a traditional bow, this weapon had to be cocked back all the way. But also unlike a bow, cocking it meant locking it. Which meant I didn't have to strain when lining up the perfect shot!

THK!

Then . . .

"Krhrorrr!"

They all turned, including Summer.

"Just keep goin'!" I called over the approaching gang. "I'll meet you at the path!"

I think she shouted something like, "How are you going to do that?" but not only couldn't I hear her over the cacophony of snorts, I wouldn't have had an answer for her anyway. Again, a half-formulated plan.

Phase one was pretty well devised, though, and that was how to stop the oncoming threat. It had to do with how soul sand burned, and with the worn flint and steel in my pack.

You guessed it—a barrier of blue flame.

Running along the edge of the brownish, wavy sand, I set each square alight until the C-shaped tool finally clinked out of existence.

"Yeah, that's right!" I taunted, as the snarling, grunting group halted at the whitish blue line. "What ya gonna do? Huh? What ya gonna do?"

I got my answer with a crossbow arrow in the chest.

"Message received," I oofed, then backed up into the "safety" of the ruins.

That was right about the time I realized, too late, that going through the infested bastion was the only clear way to join Summer.

"Me and my grand plans," I griped, retreating through the black brick hallway.

I made it back to the lava, came face-to-face with a piglin brute, and chopped him backward into the flaming floor. Then I confronted the real challenge.

If you found the book I left on the island, you'll recall how, when my first house was burning down, the only way to stop the lava from my tub was to release the glass-enclosed water above it. And if you haven't read it, now you know. Anyway, to do that,

I had to try to lay some dirt "stepping-stones" across the flowing fire. Unfortunately, I didn't make it all the way and nearly burned alive—a lesson that is now burned into my brain for all time.

And here I was again, only this time the dirt was black stone, and there seemed to be just enough cubes to maybe, *maybe*, hop to the central island and over to the other side.

"No way," I huffed, then turned back to hopefully find a staircase up to another floor.

"Hhrrurrhh!" More piglins from the top floor, making their way down toward me.

I took a half-step back and a deep, possibly last, breath and leapt onto the first stone.

Made it!

Only six more to go.

THK! An arrow in my shoulder, almost knocking me into the lava. A skeleton on the catwalk above, daring me to shoot back.

I cocked the crossbow and took aim, but had to quickly raise my shield to deflect its next blow, before I gave back what I'd just been given. As the skeleton toppled down for a burn bath, I hopped to the second block, then the third. Fourth. Fifth. I almost skidded off the sixth one, then braced myself for the jump to the island.

I landed hard just as a hopping magma cube landed on me. I swung upward, chopped it back into several smaller cubes, then ran to the chest to see if there was anything I could use. I found four blocks of gold, three of iron, and a diamond pickaxe that glowed with the same mysterious light I'd seen on some of the zombie pigmen's weapons.

The tool tingled in my hand, as if it was electrified. And when I reached up to smash the hanging spawner, it disintegrated the target in just one swipe.

"Whoa," I breathed, slipping this amazing, magical tool in my belt . . .

. . . right next to the fireproof potion.

Which I'd forgotten I had!

Which I didn't need anymore!

Because I could now see that this side of the little island was connected to the other side by a black stone bridge. I ran across quickly and discovered that it ended against a solid wall. But that wouldn't stop me. I attacked it with the shimmering pickaxe.

It had to be magic. There was no other explanation. It went through the various materials almost like they weren't there.

I burst out of the bastion and onto ground that felt firmer and easier to run on than soul sand, and my heart leapt at the sight of a distant, quartz cube.

"Summer!" I shouted, running toward her with my new prize held aloft. "Look what I found!"

"Lovely," she answered as I ran, panting, up beside her. "You can tell me all about it on the way."

"Don't you realize what this means?" I wheezed, as we booked it down the quartz cube path. "Magic items exist in this world! That means we can figure out how to do it ourselves! How to . . . magicify . . . other tools and weapons and—"

"And we won't get a chance to do any of that," Summer wheezed back, "if we don't get to the ruddy portal."

In the distance, across the plains, there was a purple glow. "And there it is!" I shouted.

Salvation.

Home.

"Wehwehwoowoo."

We halted, aghast, as a ghast rose up slowly behind the portal.

"You gotta be kiddin' me!" I raged as the screeching bomber fired.

"Here we go again." Summer, calm once more, casually sidestepping the explosive shell.

The ghast floated over the portal, closing in on our position.

"Try to distract it!" called Summer as she nocked an arrow to her bowstring.

It flew. Hit, but didn't do enough damage to kill.

"Gordon Bennett," she grunted. "Didn't draw back far enough."

"No problem, partner!" I cocked my crossbow, took careful aim. We shot at the same time, and, believe you me, I'd love to take credit for what happened next. Our shots met, in midair!

"Woo!" I cheered as the cannonball turned back for its living launcher.

It missed, unfortunately, but the brief respite allowed me to nock another arrow—my last arrow—into place. The ghast was moving away, forcing me to angle high.

"Bing, bang, boom," I whispered, and sent my sharp shaft soaring.

Up and toward its target . . . and down . . . down . . . right into the face of a pig zombie!

Oops?

As a group, they all turned toward us.

Summer glanced at me, sighed, then turned back to the on-coming horde and shouted, "Charge!"

Running, weapons up, we crashed into them with a rousing roar. A storm of blades and blows. Shields, armor, flesh. Cries of pain and the stink of burnt bacon in my nose.

Too many, pushing us back, blocking the way.

"Brrreee!"

The explosion threw me forward, and I landed in a pile of hovering debris.

"Guy! It's open!" Summer's voice from behind, pointing my eyes ahead.

The portal, so close. And clear all the way!

"Go!"

Up and running, eyes fixed on bouncing purple.

Just a few more steps!

"Brrreee!"

The explosion, behind me, throwing me into the gate.

Nausea, blindness.

Gray stone!

Clean cool air!

"Summer!" I turned, "We made—"

An axe swiping for my face.

A piglin brute?! It must've followed me through the gate!

Another strike, blocked by my shield, shoving me back out of the portal chamber and into the garden. Too far to hit the iron door lock. Another strike, another step backward. This time I countered with a sword slash, feeling the impact. I retreated a few steps, giving myself more room to swing.

And those few paces apart allowed me to see that something

was wrong with my attacker. It was shaking . . . and whimpering? Was it in pain? Something beyond my blow?

"Hey," I said, forgetting who I was talking to, "you okay?"

My answer was a raised axe.

I took the blow, ready to hit back . . . but didn't realize I was standing just at the edge of the pond. I fell in, and a familiar thought leapt into my head.

Drowning!

Summer had warned me. The lava cubes underneath! The bubbles wouldn't let me swim! Trapped on the bottom, feet scalding, lungs choked by boiling water.

Reaching for the edge. Too high!

Hands to the side, digging out steps. Climbing. Hacking. Bracing for another blow.

It never came.

The porcine brawler didn't move.

I was just in time to see the last of the purple bubbles pop over its now rotted face. And I suddenly realized that what I thought had been the shaking pain was actually a transformation.

"Summer, look," I chuckled, stepping right into its stinking face. "The surface world zombifies piglins! Summer?"

She wasn't there. She hadn't made it through the portal!

"Summer!"

Back into the swirl, ready to rush to her aid.

Stop!

I teetered at the edge of the floating island. That last ghast had blown away the narrow netherrack bridge!

And on the other side . . .

"Guy!"

Summer, fighting for her life, surrounded by zombie pig-men!

"I'm comin', buddy!" Backing up to jump.

Running, leaping . . .

Falling!

Lava!

Think!

Potion!

The fireproof elixir, from belt to hand to lips just as I hit the orange agony.

For a moment, I was blind and burning. Then . . . nothing!

That's right. Nothing.

Underwater, or, more accurately, underlava. Still unable to see anything but magma. But I wasn't burning anymore. I was okay!

Summer!

Swimming for the surface, popping up to see the cliff rising high above.

I could hear her, as well as the snorts of the zombified piglins attacking her.

"Summer!" I called, swimming for the bank. How to get up?

My new super-pickaxe!

It devoured netherrack with blinding speed. I was almost up when the blocks fell away to more lava!

Don't panic!

I dove in and swam up. The potion was still working as I rose to the lava pocket's roof. How long did I have? How long before the protection wore off?

Into the crunchy ceiling. Digging, climbing.

I burst up right in the middle of them, swinging my pickaxe like a madman!

"You all right?!" asked Summer, chopping at the closest undead face. "That nasty spill you took . . ."

"I meant what I said." Fighting behind her, the comfort of my back against hers. "I will never leave you again!"

Swinging for the nearest Z-pig, knocking it aside and opening a clear path to the portal.

"C'mon!" I called. "You first this time!"

Guarding our escape, I made sure that Summer got safely to the edge.

"Guy . . ." she started.

"No problem!" I backed up again. "There's more room to pick up speed! We can jump farther than I could from the other side!"

"Wehwehwoowoo!"

Behind, the pig pack, opening up to shoot.

"Jump!" I called. "We can make it!"

The sound of an incoming ghast missile.

"I'm not sure we—"

The piglins were closing in.

"JUMP!"

EPILOGUE

"Well, that's it," I said, laying the last square of red dust, "we're done."

"Well, come on down then," called Summer. "Let's give it a go."

I stepped back from the final open section of crawl space and climbed down the ladder next to Summer. She punched out the final torch, and, for a moment, we stood in absolute darkness.

"You do the honors." That was her.

"Nah." That was me. "It's your show."

"I insist," Summer pushed, "just like you insisted that we finish the job."

She had me there.

I reached back up to the simple wooden lever. How many times had I passed it, resisting the urge, until now? Heart racing, sighing deeply . . .

"Bing bang boom."

FLICK.

And night turned into day. The main chamber's entire ceiling lit up with hundreds of redstone lamps, all wired together, all at our command.

For a moment neither of us spoke, just admiring the sheer scope of our accomplishment. It had taken over a month, going back to gather all of Summer's previously stored glowstone, then mining new natural deposits to boot. And now we were finished. Every room was lit—well, almost every room. The mushroom and nether wart farms did better in darkness. But every other space was lit with the flick of a lever.

"Brill?" I asked my partner.

Summer nodded back. "Brill."

"What do you think, B.B.?" I called down to our new roommate. B.B., short for Bacon Bits, didn't respond. The zombie pigman just wandered around aimlessly, as he'd done since that first day of our aborted battle. It hadn't been so bad, sharing the mountain with a stinking, snorting deady. He was harmless and, other than that time I'd forgotten to close my bedroom door and had woken up to find him standing over me, it was kinda nice to have someone else to fill all this empty space.

And now he'd be my replacement. Summer's new partner when we said our final goodbye. We'd both known this moment would come, and, at least on my side, it had filled me with no amount of sadness. Every night, after working on our grand project, as I was alone in my room writing all this story down, I'd dreaded writing "The End." Not of our friendship, no more than with Moo and the island sheep. We'd still be connected in our hearts and minds.

Friendship cancels distance. Not the other way around.

But like with the island, this was the end of another chapter of my journey. Painful, but necessary. Necessary, but still painful.

What to say now? How to part without tears?

I'd rehearsed half a dozen speeches, each more eloquent than the last. But as I mentally fumbled for the right one, Summer spoke first with a sigh. "Well, I guess this means we're off then."

Wait? What?

"We?"

"Of course," Summer huffed. "That is, after we've packed and set everything right for the next traveler. And you have to write the last chapter of this book, don't you?" As I fumbled for a response, she continued, "And perhaps I could add a bit at the end. Your prized list of friendship lessons? That applies to me too, doesn't it?" I was speechless. She turned to shout down to B.B., "And you have to remember to leave the lights on, or else some baddies might spawn in the dark."

"Whoa . . . wha . . ." Still struggling for words. "You're coming with me?!"

"Of course!" Summer repeated, and laughed that warm summer laugh. "I thought you knew that? I thought we had an understanding."

"Well . . . I . . ."

"Sorry, that's on me, then." Another light, angelic chuckle. "I still have to work on my communication, don't I? Fresson twelve: Friends communicate."

And before I could mumble out any more mush, she looked into my eyes and said, "I should have been very clear that I won't let us be broken apart ever again." She glanced out at the main chamber, or, more precisely, the unseen land beyond. "I wonder what we'll find out there," she mused, "but I'm sure it's nothing we can't handle. Friends are stronger together." Turning back to me, her fist rose to meet mine. "Because that's what we are."

Friends.

WHAT *WE* HAVE LEARNED FROM

THE WORLD OF MINECRAFT

And I say "we" because I, Summer, am writing this bit. And it pains me to say that Guy, bless him, has made an utter pig's ear of his fresson numbers! The first official one ought to be the one he learned before meeting me, but since he's so eager to get going, we don't have time to go back and renumber them all. Therefore, I shall begin with:

Fresson 0. Friends keep you sane.

Right then: Off we go.

1. **Friendship must be earned.**

2. **Friends listen.**

3. **Friends respect each other's property.**

4. Friends keep their promises.

5. Friends respect each other's way of doing things.

6. Friends only have to apologize once.

7. Friends trust each other.

8. Friends shouldn't be afraid to admit their fears.

9. Friends take care of each other.

10. Friends are stronger together.

11. Friends respect each other's life choices.

12. Friends communicate.

13. Friends aren't afraid to be honest with friends.

14. Friends respect each other's beliefs.

15. Friends shouldn't be afraid to ask friends for help.

16. Friendship shouldn't force you to give up you.

17. Friends shouldn't part in anger.

18. Friendship cancels distance. Not the other way around.

19. Friends can fight, and they can also make up.

20. Friends don't leave friends behind. (Thank you, Guy.)

ACKNOWLEDGMENTS

To the folks at Mojang for letting me play in their sandbox.

To everyone at Del Rey, (especially Sarah Peed) who continue to prove that all great efforts are team efforts.

To Summer's primary dialog coach, Prof. Tracey Walters.

And, as always, to my amazing wife, Michelle, for more love, encouragement, advice, and support than I could ever deserve.

ABOUT THE AUTHOR

MAX BROOKS is a senior nonresident fellow at the
Modern War Institute at West Point and the Atlantic
Council's Brent Scowcroft Center for Strategy and
Security. His bestselling books include *Minecraft:
The Island*, *Devolution*, *The Zombie Survival Guide*,
and *World War Z*, which was adapted into a 2013
movie starring Brad Pitt. His graphic novels include
The Extinction Parade, *G.I. Joe: Hearts and Minds*,
and the #1 *New York Times* bestseller *The Harlem
Hellfighters*.

maxbrooks.com
Facebook.com/AuthorMaxBrooks
Twitter: @maxbrooksauthor